HEARTS ALIGNING

A Saint's Grove Novel

by

Miranda Hardy

saint's grove

Quixotic Publishing LLC
Royal Palm Beach, FL 33411
www.quixoticpublishing.com

Edited by: Todd Barselow, Keith B. Darrell
Cover by: Najla Qamber

Hearts Aligning / Miranda Hardy. — First Edition

ISBN 978-1-939588-15-9 (print edition)
ISBN 978-1-939588-14-2 (eBook)

For Gloria, My Mother

Saint's Grove Novels

Chapter One
The Event

The dust flutters in the small stream of light beaming into the basement, as I open the box that kicks off my start to a new life. "Out with the old, and in with the new," I whisper in the empty darkness. "A few boxes down here and I'll move on to scrubbing and packing up my tiny apartment upstairs. Thank goodness Grandpa wasn't a pack rat."

This place always scared me when I was younger, and as far as I knew Grandpa never used it, so I was surprised to find anything down here. The realtor said I should be sure everything was prepared before I listed the bar for sale, so I decided to venture into the dark, dank abyss to clean. "I can't believe it's been almost five years without him."

"Are you talking to yourself again?" Faith calls out from the top of the stairs.

"Maybe," I bite my lower lip and smile. "Are you spying on me again?"

"Ellie, I'm a much better spy than that. If I wanted to

spy on you, I wouldn't be asking you a question. I'd be hiding in a dark corner and you'd never know I was there." She places her hands on her hips and tilts her head side to side. She's always a bit on the dramatic side.

"Yeah, okay, whatever." I giggle and smile, knowing Faith could never be silent long enough to spy on anyone. That's what I love about her. I don't have to say much around her. She dominates every conversation and it never feels like I'm forcing myself to pretend to be interested in what she has to say. Making friends was never my forte. I think she might be my only one, actually. She will probably be the only one I'll miss…well, maybe Eddie and one other.

"You don't know me as well as you think, Ellie Whitaker." I believe she winks since the side of her smile curves upward, but it's hard to tell in the dim light.

"Shouldn't you be working in the bar instead of bugging me while I'm cleaning out the chilly, scary basement?"

"No one is here but drunk Richard, and you promised I could leave early to get ready for tonight," Faith whines.

"What's tonight?" I flip through the papers in the box, all brown sealed envelopes with different dates on them.

"I swear sometimes you live in this damn basement. You know, the 'Evening Beneath the Stars'; everyone's been talking about it for weeks." I picture her eyes rolling at my forgetfulness.

"Oh, yeah, that's right. Sorry, I forgot." I glance back down at the envelopes. It's wills. Grandpa's wills. A lot of them, all different dates. So weird. "I'll be up in a minute."

"Okay, but don't take too long." She turns and walks a

few steps up to the bar's kitchen.

"What is this?" I whisper. Talking to myself is a bad habit. No wonder people in town think I'm odd. "Odd Ellie is talking to herself again."

I shrug and open the first envelope. It's his will all right. I remember Grandpa's last wishes well, although I never quite understood what he was thinking when he wrote it. He knew I didn't want to come back, and I certainly didn't want to run the bar when he was gone.

The bar was left to me in trust and I was required to run it and live in the apartment. The only difference between this will and the final one the lawyer gave me is the date. The final will required me to stay here five years, but this one says six. Once that period was up, the bar would be mine, free and clear, along with $1,500,000. At that time I could do with it as I like. If I chose not to run the bar for that long, then I'd get nothing and the money would go to the town for historical preservation purposes.

Grandpa knew I'd stay for the money. It'll help me continue my schooling, pay off my student loans, and move away from this suffocating small town. For the first few years, I resented his request. I still don't understand why he made these conditions. He knew what I wanted. How did he save up that much money? We practically lived like paupers. He was always working...seven days a week, never taking a vacation the entire time I grew up. It was maddening.

I open the next envelope. Same will, only seven years to own the bar. The next is one more year. This box is full of his wills, all dated the year before the last and each requiring I run the bar for an additional year. My mind buzzes with confusion.

"Are you coming?" Faith yells from the kitchen.

"Coming!" I grab the box to bring upstairs so I can rummage through it some more and rid myself of yet another distraction.

Faith walks away through the kitchen, her heels click on the tile as I climb the stairs. I tug the dangling string to turn off the single bare bulb in the basement while balancing the box between my hip and the wall to keep it from falling. Dust flies into my face as I turn to push the door shut with my butt.

Blinking continuously to shake the dust from my eyes, I hit a cement wall and scream. Once my vision clears, I see it's not cement, only Eddie. "Jesus, Eddie, you scared me."

"That's what I'm here for, ma'am." He grabs the box from me with ease and takes it out of the kitchen, setting it on the bar.

"Thanks." I wipe my face off with a bar towel. "I swore I hit a friggin' brick wall."

"I get that all the time." Eddie doesn't crack a smile. He never does. His lips don't turn upward at all…ever. I think the Navy scared the smile right out of him when he was younger. I try to imagine a young Eddie…forty years ago, entering the service. I wonder if he had more hair, or if it was always shaved? I picture a tall, thin young man, looking sharp in a newly-pressed uniform. I shake my head…he probably didn't smile then either.

He takes off his apron and hangs it on the hook inside the kitchen. "Are you sure you'll be okay by yourself?" He's taken over the role of 'father figure' since Grandpa died. We have the 'no family' trait in common now.

Several years ago his dad died of a heart attack, and his mother died of a broken heart a year later, or at least that's how he tells it. He was an only child, too.

"Oh yeah, no problem." I look around the dead bar. Drunk Richard's head lays on his arm. He's probably passed out again. "I think I can manage. Besides, Faith is coming back after the lunar eclipse to help out in case it gets busy. I'll cook and she'll serve…the usual." Faith is nowhere in sight. "Where is she?"

"Upstairs." He heads toward the door.

No doubt rummaging through my boring clothes for a gem she can steal. "Bye, Eddie." I wave.

"See you tomorrow." My one cook, who's been working at the bar for over twenty years, leaves me alone. The bell hanging over the front door jingles as Eddie leaves for the night. It still puzzles me why he requested the night off. I didn't picture him as one who would enjoy the 'Evening Beneath the Stars'.

The front door swings shut, shaking that darn bell again, and my attention returns to the dusty box lingering on the bar. "Oh Man! I should have asked him about the stupid wills. He probably knows more about Grandpa than I do."

"Talking to yourself again, I see." Faith enters through the public bathroom hall that also leads to the door to the upstairs apartment…my apartment. One of my flowery tops hangs over her arm. "Unless you're talking to Drunk Richard, but I don't think he can hear you."

"Ha, ha!" I give her a half-smile.

"What wills?" She comes over to the box, and taking it upon herself, looks inside. "Yuck…dusty."

"Yeah. I guess my grandfather redid his will every year." Faith thumbs through them and takes the envelopes out. A picture stuck between two envelopes falls onto the bar. She grabs it away as I reach for it.

"Wow! She's beautiful." Faith admires the old-looking print.

I snatch it from her and look at a photograph of my dad with his arm around a beautiful brunette in front of a cabin in the woods.

Faith steps next to me to look at the picture again. "Is that your mother?"

"I don't know," I answer truthfully. I've never seen an image of my mother. Grandpa said he never had one, but he described her as beautifully as the woman in this picture. "I think it is."

A tear trickles down my right cheek and I wipe it clear. Did Grandfather lie? He had to know it was in here since he kept his wills in this box, replacing them each year.

"Her eyes are mesmerizing, like diamonds against an icy blue backdrop. How come you never told me your dad was so gorgeous?"

"I never knew either of them." Faith knows this. I wish she wouldn't ask about things she already knows.

"Look." She nods toward the door before it opens and Bryan Nichols walks in.

Faith takes her apron off and throws it in her box under the bar faster than a rabbit running from a hunter.

"Faith, can you?" My eyes widen and I motion toward Bryan, now sitting in his usual table by the front window, furthest from the bar itself.

She holds her hands up and moves swiftly to the door.

"I'm off, Ellie. See you after the eclipse." She smiles as I narrow my eyes. She's doing this on purpose, knowing I hate dealing with him. It's not that I hate him. It's that he obviously hates me. He never says more to me than to give me his order, which is how it's been these last couple of months. He never said anything to me in high school, either. Some people don't change, even after five years.

I take a deep breath and walk over. He's early today. Usually, he doesn't come in until 10:00…every night like clockwork. I look at the clock and it's right before 9:00. He must have gotten off work early.

"The usual?" I left my pad and pen on the bar; he won't order food. He never does. He nods and looks back out the window toward the grassy town square.

Okay then. Sometimes I feel like it's high school all over and everyone ignores me—like I don't exist…one of the reasons I was so happy to leave for my first semester of college. It was a chance at a different life, a town so far from Saint's Grove, away from where I was nobody. If I had been more outgoing, that first semester would have been different. I still enjoyed college—the big library, no one giving me weird glances…no one knowing me as the strange, quiet girl. Everyone was into his or her studies, or partying… Completely different from high school. So much life and so much to do there. And then Grandpa died and I had to quit and come back.

Pouring his beer from the tap, I think about how Bryan was in high school—entirely the opposite of me. He was the outgoing, popular star. Every girl adored him, and every guy was envious, I'm sure. He was so athletically inclined and seemed to enjoy being out on the field. He smiled all the time. I miss that grin. He went away to college, too, but was able to finish his degree. He's only been back two months, working as a graphic designer at Richards Industries. I haven't seen that winning smile once in that time, but he's been in every day. He seems miserable now; a tale must lay behind those sorrowful eyes that no one can break from him.

Even when Shawn, his best friend in high school, comes in, they ignore each other. I'm sure there's a story there, too, but I'm so oblivious I hear nothing. You'd think I'd hear it all in the bar, but it's mostly petty gossip that circles my ears, like who's cheating on whom, and who has what money woes.

I take his beer and set it down quietly in front of him. He nods. "Thanks."

"You're welcome." I linger. "You're not going to the 'Evening Beneath the Stars'?"

He shakes his head. "Nah." He gazes up at me for a split second. His eyes used to be so much brighter. Now they are the color of wet grass after the rain. It's as if they've darkened. Is that possible?

"Okay, well if you need anything." I point toward the bar and move backward, hitting the chair at the table behind me. Real smooth, Ellie. I turn, but I could have sworn I glimpsed the tiniest movement of his mouth…almost a smile, but not quite.

I want to curse and hit myself in the head over and over, but that would make me seem even more awkward.

Trying to keep busy and occupy my mind with anything other than the hunky Bryan sitting in the corner thinking I'm a complete loser, I take out the remaining wills and flip through them to be sure I'm not missing anything. At the bottom of the box is a crumbled up piece of yellowed paper.

Bryan's chair scratches against the wood floor as he gets up, places his money on the table, and heads for the door. He turns to face me. "Thanks, Ellie. See you tomorrow."

He leaves. I wave, my hand frozen in the air, my mouth hanging open. Five words…he actually said five words to me and one of them was my name. He knows my name.

I put my hand down, a few moments after he leaves, realizing there's a big, stupid smile on my face now. I shake my head to clear these ridiculous, foolish thoughts. "Get it together, Ellie. You're not a damn teenager anymore."

I grab the crumbled paper from the box to throw it away, but decide to unwrap it to see if it's anything important. It's in Grandpa's writing.

"Dear Ellie, I've lied to you your entire life and I'm sorry." That's all it says.

Chapter Two
The Event

The unfinished note seems to disintegrate in my hand, with the moisture from my tears smearing the few words it contains. My shaky hand places the crumbled paper on the bar top and I take a deep breath, wiping my face. What had he lied about?

Drunk Richard's head pops up, his forehead red from the imprint of his arm. "I'll have another, Ellie." He points to his empty beer glass.

"Richard, you're barely awake. Why don't you head home, or maybe into the square to see the planets align?" I hope he'll leave early so I can be alone with my thoughts.

"Come on, Ell, please, one more for the road." His browned teeth peek under his goofy, crooked smile.

"One more and off you go." I pour his drink and set it in front of him, taking his old glass from the bar.

long ago. I pour two beers, then
don't order any food as I bring th

"Thanks," Mitch says. Shav
seen my boy tonight?" Mitch lc
where Bryan, his son, had sat.

"He left twenty minutes ago
the empty seat. "Anything else?"

"No, thanks," Mitch answers
for an instant too long, a disdain
don't think he ever liked me mu
don't think he even knows we g
ass. "He was early tonight," Mitc

I go back to the bar and br
into the kitchen to wash later. I
since Eddie is off. I dread these
hope Faith does come back to he

Another patron walks in,
Saint's Grove attracts tourists th
the architecture. It's a nice sp
away from the busy cities. It's fi
flock here to vacation and I feel

The newcomer stares at Mi
appear oblivious, for a little too
contemplating whether he wants

"Can I help you?" I smile at
His gaze shifts to me and l

dark hair falls a little over his left brown eye. It seems to sparkle under the fluorescent light. He walks to the bar and sits on the closest stool. "Do you have anything other than fried food?"

"We have sandwiches." I hand him a menu and hope he doesn't ask for me to make one.

He takes it, but doesn't look at it. "You seem to be an interesting character. I'm Desmon." He tilts his head again and squints as if studying me. I feel as if I'm a piece of art in a museum. "I think you should come home with me." He holds out his hand inviting me to go with him... Well, isn't that presumptuous?

"Umm...I don't think so, but thanks." I raise my eyebrows. The full moon must be attracting all the crazies tonight. He's cute, but also a bit too creepy for my tastes.

"What are you?" He pulls his hand slowly back. He scrunches his nose, shocked I didn't take his hand.

"Ellie?" Mitch waves his empty mug. I quickly fill two more glasses and carry them to their table, glad to be elsewhere.

When I return to the bar, the stranger, Desmon exits abruptly. Is this going to be a night full of oddness?

The bell sounds again, and Faith pokes her head in. "It's about to start." She throws me some cheap binoculars. I miss them and they fall into the sink, splashing soapy water onto the bar. "Good catch." She laughs.

"Thanks." I roll my eyes.

"I'll be back later." Faith pops out again.

Wiping the bar, I hear the door open and half expect it to be Faith returning to chastise my catching skills, but it's Bella from the bakery.

I wave. "Hey, Bella. Are you open tonight?" She makes the best muffins I've ever tasted, one of the few things I would miss about this town.

She nods. "I was. What about you? Have you been busy?"

"A bit. Some strangeness in the air, I think. What can I get for you?" I ask, but I can guess what she'd like.

Bella leans over the counter. "Vodka and tonic. Can I get it in a to-go cup? I'm going back to the store in a little bit to clean up."

I smile. I knew exactly what she wanted. She's not a big drinker, but she has her favorite. "You've got it."

"Have you seen it? The planets?" She points her thumb toward the door.

The darkened sky looms and I shake my head. "Not yet. I'll peek out in a while, I'm sure." I hand her the drink and she pays, leaving me her usual generous tip.

"Thanks." She smiles and heads out the door. I wave.

"We have to find him." Shawn stands from his chair. Mitch nods, throws down enough bills to pay for the drinks, and they walk out without a word.

I know Mitch and Shawn work together in the mines, but it seems odd that Mitch hangs out with his son's old best friend. Perhaps he was a father figure to him as well.

Drunk Richard snores, his head firmly resting on his arm again.

"Jesus! Seriously?" I say aloud to no one. I'm tempted to throw water on him to rouse him, but decide it's a good time to peek out to see what all the fuss is about, seeing as it's what everyone's been talking about for weeks. Besides, it's not every day you see six planets align, followed by a lunar eclipse.

Stepping outside, I realize the binoculars Faith threw at me lay on the counter. Oh well, I'm sure I won't need them. Many people have gathered. Families sit with their children on blankets, which reassures me they won't be visiting the bar for a drink afterward. There are familiar faces throughout the crowd. I even see the mountain-woman, Brickell, at the back of the grassy square, an unusual sight as she rarely comes to town, but I can't see Faith.

As I watch the families gathered, I wonder if I'll ever be one of those women with a family whose husband packs up their picnic dinner and they lay beneath the sky watching the stars, smiling and laughing. It seems too farfetched. That would require a 'normal' man to notice I exist…and for that man to like me in that way. It all seems so impossible. I never had a mother and father sitting with me under the stars, and I imagine Grandpa, if he were still alive, would be inside the bar and not wasting his time out here with all of these 'foolish people.'

Even with the moonlight so bright, it's still difficult to see who is where, but one face seems more familiar than any other. Bryan stands on the other side of the grassy town square, in front of the hair salon, 'A Little Off the Top.' It dawns on me the reason I recognize him is everyone else's gaze looks up, but he's not staring at the sky. Our eyes meet for a split second and then sparks in my peripheral vision take my gaze away.

I look up and see the full moon turning red as the Earth's shadow covers it through the reflection of the sun. The moon overshadows the other planets in alignment: Earth, Mars, Venus, Jupiter, Saturn and Mercury. One of the first college courses I took during my one and only semester included Astronomy and we discussed both lunar and solar eclipses. I didn't think much of it at that time, but seeing it happen doesn't do the descriptions I studied justice.

The blood moon looks as if a hand is gently squeezing the top and the blood pumps toward the bottom of the round sphere. The orangish-red color is so much brighter on the bottom, with darkened gray shadows spotting the top. I don't think I've ever seen the moon so large.

As if it were going to cry its amazing color onto us, sparks illuminate the sky. It starts directly below the moon and branches out into the sky. "Oohs" and "aahs" murmur, echoing through the town square. I can't keep my eyes from the sky. Meteors descend to Earth from the direction in which the moon and the planets align.

These aren't the typical meteors seen in previous

night skies. These appear more vibrant in color and larger, closer to the Earth as if they've decided to breach the Earth's atmosphere at incredible speeds. There are bursts of purples and blues, yellow and orange hues, and even some speckled silver tails trailing some of the meteors. I wish I could capture this on video to watch over and over. No one would ever believe this if they were not here to witness such an experience.

My ears ring, followed by an annoying hum, like a loud dinner bell's vibration playing on a loop. It won't stop. I grab my ears and look away from the sky. I pull and push on my ears, but the sound won't cease. I look around to see other people, assuming they are hearing the same thing, but no one else is cupping their ears. They are smiling at the bright stars falling from the sky. I see lips moving, but I can't hear words escaping anyone's mouth.

A giant, thick fog pierces the night from the center of the town square, near the statue of Peter Saint. It goes unnoticed by many seated in the square since they still peer up at the falling stars.

A vibrational sonic boom hits me, knocking me against the bar window. The ringing subsides and immediate surrounding noises penetrate my eardrums once more, but they seem much louder, as if everyone is screaming. That's when I notice people *are* screaming. Distressing sounds of terror erupt all around the town square. Fogs gush from all over the grassy square, as if someone has opened a number of large freezers and the cold temperature has met with the warm night air.

At certain places light trails the fogginess, and the screams soon follow. My eyes are drawn to one light spot across the grass, in front of the florist's door. I see Faith there, her gaze set to the opening where a bright light pushes through the darkness. Out steps one of the strangest creatures I've ever seen. It's a reptilian-looking creature standing upright and dressed in metal armor. What the hell?

He's looking at Faith and raises an archaic weapon with a sharp circular blade on the end of it.

"Oh my god!"

Screams erupt from all over the square, and people run in every direction.

I want to run to Faith and protect her, but I'll never beat the reptile running toward her. Faith doesn't look frightened. She raises her hands to him, her lips move as if she's speaking to him. He freezes as he's about to lower his weapon on her; literally freezes. Ice covers his body as if she had frozen him with her words. Faith backs up and looks around. She sees me staring at her, hands covering my mouth. She turns and runs toward the screams in the darkness, not away from it like most people in the town square.

People flee from the dense patches of fog where creatures emerge from the colorless gap; beings of different species I've never seen before in my life. Our calm, boring town has erupted into a Stephen King nightmare. Winged men and women in white robes carrying swords descend from the sky in different places where several of the strange creatures appeared. Angels? It can't be.

Fifty feet away, an opening appears in the fog and a humanoid figure walks out. He looks human, but then he jumps onto a running man and sinks large fangs into the side of his neck.

I look for Faith, but she's nowhere in the darkness that I can see, but I spot Bryan standing a hundred feet away. His jaw is slightly open and his eyes are bright and bulging; he watches me with an emotion I had never seen in him before. It's fear. He mouths something at me, but I can't make out his words with the chaotic noise around me. He points to the portal the creatures emerge from and that's when I see the fanged man staring at me.

His dark hair and pale skin are familiar...from horror movies and books. He's a vampire. A fictional creature made up to scare us or entice us, whatever the stupid story calls for at the time of its popularity. "This can't be real." I shake my head. He's finished off the man he attacked, the poor guy's body limp on the grass, and stares at me with a hunger I've never seen before. This isn't the kind vampire who takes pity on the poor innocent, naive girl. No, this vampire is the one from nightmares, and it looks like he's chosen his next victim—me.

Chapter Three
The Event

Time slows and my heartbeat booms in my ear like a pounding drum. Instinct tells me to run, but my feet won't budge. They've given up before starting, knowing there is no way in hell I can outrun this beast that races toward me faster than humanly possible. I brace and pray it's a quick death and not too painful.

The vampire bares his bloodstained fangs. I lean back placing my arms out in front of me. A large rustic white and brown wolf smashes into the vampire. They crash into the bar door, shattering the glass. I back away from the flying shards, but several slice through my arm. It feels like a hundred needles pinching me at once.

The door hangs by one of its hinges, swaying. The bell that was attached to the top of the door clanks as it hits the ground. I crouch and peer through the large window and see the wolf clamp down on the vampire's neck. He thrashes from side to side, ripping into the pale skin. Blood gushes, dousing the wolf with its thick darkness. The vampire's mouth opens wide as if he's screaming, but no sound comes out. He scratches at the wolf, but can't grab hold of his body. The vampire's arms fall to his sides and his body goes limp in the wolf's grasp.

Another scream pulls my attention toward the grassy square. In the darkness, bodies entwine themselves in bloody dances, like shadows behind red curtains. Howls echo through the night, but it's not from the wolf in my bar. That wolf drags the vampire out onto the sidewalk and flings it into the street. He turns his attention to the darkness before us and growls.

Red beady eyes blink behind the blackness. The wolf backs into me, bumping me toward the bar door, as if herding me. Then the red beady eyes come closer and they are attached to a rather hefty body topped with thick spiral-shaped horns. Its face is beastly-looking with a large snout squashed into its face. There's no hair on its head; the spiral horny antlers, one on each side of its circular orifice, make up the top of the creature. I've never seen this in a Stephen King movie.

"Okay." I back into the bar, but the beady eyes follow my every move. That's when the wolf pounces at the towering horned figure, and I retreat further into the bar. The door swings on its single hinge, but I try to shut it the best I can, pushing it closed with all my might.

For some reason, I feel safe inside here, as if nothing out there can get to me in here, but that's a foolish notion, isn't it? I look at the door's missing window.

"Well, my slogan-laced front door window is gone. I guess it's no longer 'happy hour every hour' here. I guess I can now add no animals or vampires to the no shirt, no shoes, no service policy when I redo the window." A sick nervous laugh escapes me. "How do you explain this to the insurance company? Excuse me, sir, but my window and door were smashed in by a large wolf attacking a vampire…a vampire that was about to eat me." Great…I finally get a sense of humor in times of stressful situations, and no one's here to hear my wit.

I grab the towel I had left on the bar earlier and swab the cuts on my arm. Some shards fall to the floor. I don't think I'm badly injured, but I am scratched up. I need to wash the areas and bandage them. No big deal. No big deal.

I throw the towel back onto the bar and turn to view the interior damage—glass strewn across the floors, broken wooden chairs, one smashed table, and a lot of blood smearing the floor. That won't be easy to clean. That's when I notice Drunk Richard staring at me from under the bar, one hand tightly clutching a full mug. "I guess I wasn't talking to myself after all." I completely forgot about him being here. "Hey, did you refill that yourself?" I point toward his beer.

Drunk Richard stands, and lets the mug fall to the ground and shatter. The beer splashes my leg several feet away.

"What the hell." I want to yell at him, but his face

takes on a different look and it freaks me out. "Um, Richard, I think you need to call someone to pick you up now."

Not only is his facial expression unnerving, but a slight aura of yellow light pulses from his body, like a beacon that summons a ship to shore. I rub my eyes, thinking the color will disappear when I look again. It's still there, and now I'm sure I'm losing any ounce of sanity I had left.

"Richard, we should call Mary to fetch you now. Things are a little weird outside, and she can drive around back to pick you up in the alley." I back away slowly, his creepy stare following my every move. I take one step back toward the kitchen, and he takes one step toward me.

"You the luveliest woman I ever seen." Richard's soft, drunken voice pays me a compliment that sounds eerie coming from his dry cracked lips. "I ever told ya that?" He takes another step toward me, holding on to the side of the bar as he moves. I step back.

"No, no, I don't recall that, Richard." My voice rises an octave. I clear my throat. "How much have you had to drink exactly?"

"Well, it true though. Your eyes so beautiful, I can't keep from sturing at them." He doesn't blink, which adds to the eeriness.

"Dru...Richard, my eyes are brown, like most of the women on this planet—poop brown." I nervously smile and take a step that pushes me through the swinging door of the kitchen. I quickly survey the counter and grab the first thing I see—a spatula. That's great, a damn spatula to fend off a crazed drunkard.

He shakes his head and holds out his hand to stop the door from swinging, probably holding himself steady as well, while he intently looks at my face.

"And your hair…so bouncy and smuth." Drunk Richard continues forward. He reaches out and sweeps his hand through my hair. I swat it with the spatula, but that doesn't stop him from taking another awkward step forward.

I back up against the kitchen island with pots dangling from above, and move quickly to the side to take a few more steps back. "Richard, there's the phone right there." I point to the wall phone. "Give Mary a call, please."

He turns to look at the phone and shakes his head while returning his gaze to me.

"It you, Ellie. It always been you." He smiles that crooked goofy smile.

My back hits the wall. I'm trapped with Drunk Richard and no one to stop his advances. I'm sure it wouldn't be too hard to take him down, right? One swift kick to the groin should do it. He's wasted anyway.

"Give us a kiss, Ellie." He steps closer, pointing to his lips, and I smell the beer emanating from his body.

"I don't think that's a good idea, Richard." I want to gag at the thought of his lips touching me, but then, his stinking beer breath hits me, and something stirs inside of me...like a need for that light surrounding him to leave him and be inside me. It's not a sexual impulse, but more of a growing hunger within my center. It's the strangest feeling I've ever encountered.

Then he backs up, wobbling. His skin becomes paler by the second and the yellow light surrounding him dims and wavers...a nervous emotion. His yellow pulse speaks to me somehow...I understand it. He no longer looks at me, but gazes toward the basement door. A feeling of relief passes through me, but also one of utter disappointment. I knew that I could have somehow taken that beautiful yellow light from him.

Bryan, completely naked, flies through the door and pulls Drunk Richard backwards, away from me. He pushes him through the sliding door and out into the main bar. I rush to the door, peering through the filmy glass window of the kitchen to see Bryan fling Drunk Richard into the dark town square. I can't help but think he won't survive the chaos taking place. How could Bryan do such a thing?

Bryan...completely naked...in my bar. I need to get this window cleaned, damn it. Where the heck did his clothes go? Sweat glistens on his biceps under the light of the bar. He stands there looking at me through the window. He doesn't even try to cover up. I scan every inch of his muscular torso. I knew he was well built, but he looks much more so without being trapped in those dreary business suits he wears daily. I follow his torso down....oh my god. I feel a redness seep into my cheeks. His leg muscles gleam under the light and that's when I see his color aura. It's a brownish, chestnut color. So different from the yellow of Drunk Richard. He almost glows in the dimness. It's amazing to behold, and I want to get close to him...to touch him, and that beautiful light that illuminates his body.

His eyes bore into me and I wonder what he is thinking. This has to be a dream. The man I've admired for so many years is standing naked in my bar.

"I don't want to wake up. I don't want to wake up now."

Bryan smiles. He heard me.

"Ellie!" A booming voice yells behind me, and it's a voice I haven't heard in five years, but there's no mistaking it. The loud resonant tone only ever belonged to one person I know, or I knew. The small hairs on my neck rise and goosebumps form on my arms and legs. I turn to see the figure that belongs to the voice.

My dead grandfather hovers by the basement door, pointing downward into the dark space I was in hours before. His body seems solid, as it had been before he died. He smiles at me, winks, and looks down where he's pointing into the basement. His smile disappears and he mouths something to me I can't make out. Then poof...he disappears. He literally crumbles; his body breaks away into small fragments of air, like a pixilated screen breaking away from a full picture.

This can't be real...numbness fogs my mind and a

hum becomes louder in my ears. I feel as if my heart just slammed into my chest, ready to pop out onto the floor. Frantic, I try to find something to hold me up, as I know I'm about to fall. As I feel myself fade, strong arms wrap around my waist and I briefly see my rescuer before darkness completely takes over.

Chapter Four
Day One

The aroma of sage greets me, and I know I'm in my room since I remember picking the purple Aster wild flowers yesterday morning in the woods. Slight guilt edges in, knowing these beautiful flowers would be dead soon, since I plucked them from their home for my selfish pleasure, but winter approaches and they wouldn't have survived in the wild much longer anyway.

I stretch, kicking the blanket free from my warm body, and pat my pillow searching for my stuffed bear to snuggle. "It was only a dream, thank goodness." Bear's soft fur tickles my face when I pull it closer. I blink away the haziness of sleep and hear a rough throat clear, followed by a deep snicker. Pulling the covers over me, I look toward the corner the noise came from. I see Bryan sitting in one of my chairs grinning. "What? Um..."

My mind clears. I realize I'm in my t-shirt and undies, and my arms are bandaged. "How?"

"Want some coffee?" Bryan heads toward my tiny kitchen. Since we have a full kitchen downstairs, Grandpa didn't see the need for a large one in the apartment. "Can I get your Teddy some milk?" There it is…that smile I haven't seen since high school. For a brief moment my thoughts melt away, but reality materializes quickly reminding me I'm at home.

I sit up on the bed and toss the bear at him, not even coming close to hitting him. "What are you doing up here?" The events of last night rush back to me. "Last night wasn't a dream?"

He holds up the coffee pot and raises his eyebrows. His straight, short brown hair covers one of his eyes, and he pushes it back. His clear complexion glistens under the light brown aura. He's truly a magnificent looking man.

I shake my head. I still don't understand these colors around people. Something must be off with my eyesight. The aura moves in unison with his body. It reminds me of dancing flames on a log…the fire of a different color. "I think I'm seeing things," I mumble.

"What's that?"

"I don't drink coffee." I turn away and search my immediate area. I don't see my jeans lying around. The ones I wore last night before…before I passed out. It dawns on me: he took my bottoms off and put me in bed. I peek under the covers and see I wore my nice green sparkling bikini undies. Thank goodness I wasn't wearing my granny panties. He would have gotten a chuckle.

"Then why do you have coffee here?" Bryan sips

from the cup he poured.

"That was my Grandfather's, so it should be well aged by now." I wrap the cover around me, then take a pair of sweats from my bottom drawer. "What are you doing up here?" I make my way into the bathroom and shut the door. I pull my sweatpants on as quickly as possible and rejoin him in my living room. "Why did you undress me? You big pervert!"

He continues drinking the five-year-old coffee. Does coffee even age, or rot, or go bad? There has to be an expiration date on the package. Now Bryan probably thinks I don't clean out my cupboards, which I don't, but that's none of his damn business. Why is he even talking to me as if we're friends? My mind races with questions I can't answer.

"After you passed out last night, no one else was here to care for you, so I brought you up to bed, bandaged you...I wanted to be sure you didn't have cuts on your legs, too. You had several holes in your jeans. I'm not a pervert." He rolls his eyes and faces away, looking out the window to the woods. "I decided to stay to be sure you were safe. There was a lot of destruction around town, but your bar isn't too terribly damaged. We managed to keep the looters and, uh, others away."

"Umm, thanks, I think. I'm not quite sure what happened, but I am thankful you helped me out. You didn't have to do that, you know." I check my bandages. My arms are a little sore. "Glad to see you found your clothes, by the way." Him standing stark naked in my bar I remember well. His white, long-sleeve dress shirt hangs unbuttoned against his chest, stained with God knows what, and his navy slacks are ruined with tears along the seams.

"Yeah, uh, sorry about that." He walks to the window facing the forest.

"Can you tell me what's happening?"

He turns to me. "Can you tell me what you are?"

"Um…" I have to stop saying um like a moron all the damn time. "A girl?" My eyes bulge trying to understand his question.

"No, you're not only a girl, Ellie." The light from the window catches him at the right angle, and his chestnut aura shines brightly around him.

This is freaking me out…I'm on the verge of a major anxiety attack. I breathe deeply and clear my thoughts.

"And you're not only a graphic designer, but apparently a stripper as well." I fold my arms and tap my foot. "What do you mean I'm not only a girl. I have girl parts. I think I'd know if I wasn't. And what happened to your clothes last night? Did some creature rip them off you?" The image of the ghastly beasts returns to my mind. The reptilian-looking monster standing on two legs, the horned pig-faced giant with the red eyes, the large wolf that attacked the vampire that was going to kill me…had all this happened? I clutch the side of my sofa and sit on its edge.

"Ellie…" He pauses, and sighs. "I'm sorry about the bar door. I nailed it back up and Eddie's working on it now." I don't think that's what he wanted to say.

He bites his lip.

"What do you mean?" I ask, thinking about the large wolf attacking the vampire. "The wolf..." That's why his aura is the color of the earth on a rainy day. I don't know how I know, but I do. "You're the wolf. A werewolf?"

He nods. He looks out the window at the forest again. "And you're not only a girl."

"I think—I think I need a drink." I point toward the stairs leading to the bar and head in that direction. His footfalls aren't far behind, so I know he's following.

Another table chair leans edged up against the apartment door. I place it to the side, and unlock the door to the hall where the public bathrooms hide next to the kitchen. I thought it was sweet Bryan locked us in for the night, but also a little bizarre. Were we in that much danger? Are we still?

The bathrooms look relatively normal, and the door to the bar is unscathed. The bar is a different matter. Eddie hammers a nail latching on wood where the window used to be. Faith stops sweeping and looks at me. It's the first time I've seen her at the start of a day without a smile on her face.

Her purple aura pulses under the light from the glass window. It's a soft lilac color that brings out her beauty. It also tells me something else about her: She's not human. I can't smile at her. A million thoughts swarm through my head and confusion builds, as these colors surrounding everyone become beacons. They are both mesmerizing and scary.

One thing I know for certain...she's been hiding a secret from me for a long time. I thought she was my best friend…well, my only real friend.

"I'm a witch." She answers my unasked question, holding the broom next to her chin...how cliché.

I plop down into the closest chair and fold my hands together on the table. I take a deep breath. I glance at Eddie, whose aura is the same color as Bryan's, only not as bright from this distance. "And Eddie is a werewolf". He stops hammering and looks at me, and then at Bryan.

Faith turns to Eddie. "Eddie's a werewolf?" Her eyes narrow and I know she knew nothing about Eddie or Bryan.

I shake my head. "You never said anything to me? Either of you."

Faith drops the broom. She races to my side, plopping to her knees staring up at me. "I couldn't say anything. It's a rule we have to abide by or else we're severely punished." She slides her finger across her neck. "Would you have believed me anyway?"

"Probably not." I shake my head. "What about your secret, Eddie? Do you and Bryan know each other?"

"Bryan's a werewolf, too?" Faith asks. Bryan ignores her. He walks to the broom and picks it up, placing it against the bar.

"It's not something we go around announcing," Eddie says. "Like the little witch here, we aren't allowed to blab our secrets."

Faith scrunches her nose at him.

The roar of an ambulance makes us gaze toward the window. Faith grabs my hands. "A lot of people were hurt last night, and some damage was done, but I don't think the nightmare is over, Ellie. Maybe we should get out of town for a while." She drags a chair over while still holding my hand.

I shake my head faster. "I'm not leaving."

I pull away from Faith and peer out the window. Store windows elsewhere are smashed, too. A flipped car sits lonely on the street in front of the bar. Bodies are covered with sheets in different parts of the grassy town square. I look away from the devastation for a moment, close my eyes, breathe, and look outside again. Police patrols surround paramedic workers helping survivors. I lean into the window, staring at the statue and a misty cloud still lingers at its base.

"Ellie, the rifts…or portals haven't all closed. Things escaped into the night, and there may be more yet to come." Faith joins me.

Bryan helps Eddie with the door. They ignore our exchange, but I know they can hear everything we say.

"How long have you rehearsed this? What happened to that cute, bubbly girl who acted like a teenager?" Faith's solemnness irritates me. "I'm the grown-up here, remember?" She's 21, a couple of years younger than I am, but never acts like it. She's the one without a plan or clear vision for her future. Who can blame her? She doesn't have the responsibility to manage and own a bar at her age.

"Uhh." She sits and plops her head down on the

table closest to us. "Why are you so stubborn, Ellie Whitaker?"

"Why do you have to be such a witch?" I ask, smiling.

She peeks up. "That's not funny you know." She sits up and stares at me, as I join her at the table. "There's something different about you."

"Two werewolves and a witch walk into a bar…" I can't help myself. It sounds too strange not to say aloud.

"Omigod, really? When did you develop a sense of humor?" Faith feels my forehead. "You obviously hit your head last night when you fainted into lover boy's arms." She points to Bryan.

I shove her back into her seat. "You should have heard me right after Bryan the Werewolf busted the door attacking the vampire about to eat me, but you were too busy fighting off a giant alligator with…" I raise my hands and wave them in the air.

"Ice. I froze him, and I don't think they called themselves alligators." She crinkles her nose, looking up at the ceiling. "I believe they were some reptilian species, but still scary. He was going to chop my damn head off, can you believe that?"

I shake my head. "I can't believe I'm having this conversation. Eddie! You've worked here for more than twenty years. Did Grandpa know what you are?"

"No, ma'am, he didn't." Eddie bangs one last nail into the wooden door and steps back.

"Not too bad," Bryan says, testing it.

"We ain't no carpenters, that's for sure," Eddie

replies. "It'll do."

"Grandpa!" I stand and push the table back. Everyone looks at me. "He, uh, he was here last night. He scared Drunk Richard away. It had to be him."

"What?" Faith asks.

"Grandpa was in the kitchen, by the door. He pointed to the basement, winked, and disappeared. Why would he do that?"

Faith and I look toward the kitchen at the same time.

Chapter Five
Day One

Bryan cuts us off as we race to the kitchen. "You can't run into the dark basement like that." He signals Eddie with a brief jerk of his head. Eddie puts the hammer on the counter.

"Oh, come on. There's only a few boxes left down there," I argue. "I'm sure we can handle it."

"Like you handled the vampire last night by standing there?" He raises an eyebrow.

"Thank goodness I wasn't wearing a red cape with a hood or you might have eaten me." I take a jab at him and follow him and Eddie.

Faith giggles. She follows us into the kitchen. "Boy, Ellie, you are surprising me with the jokes this morning." She leans in. "He's got a cute butt though. Go easy on him."

I roll my eyes. "Really?"

Bryan turns around. "We can hear you, you know."

"Dogs with supersonic hearing…got it. Anything else we should know about you?" I put my hands on my hips. "Do you go around sniffing butts in your spare time? I bet you're great Frisbee players."

Eddie chuckles this time, which sounds odd coming from him. I don't think I've ever heard him laugh.

Bryan stops me as I inch toward the basement. "Had your fun? Let the adults go down and fetch your ghost's boxes. Okay, princess?"

I back off. "Okay, then." I think I offended him. I guess he's somewhat touchy about the subject.

Eddie and Bryan head down into the basement while Faith and I remain in the kitchen.

"I think you hurt his feelings." Faith pouts, sticking her bottom lip out.

"Why are you here, Faith? If it's so dangerous out there, why not get out of town and go home ?"

She shrugs. "Mom can handle herself. Our 'witchiness' runs in the family. I guess I wanted to be sure you were all right, and help here in town where I'm more useful. This bar is kind of my home away from home." She looks around. "You took me in and gave me a job when no one else in this town would give me the time of day. People can be so judgmental."

I remember the first time she came through the door three years ago, fresh out of high school. She practically bounced in, wearing a black skirt that looked like a tutu and bright purple hair. She's always remained bubbly, outgoing, and never afraid to express her uniqueness. "I miss the purple hair."

"Ah, blue is more my color." She twirls a piece in

her fingers.

Bryan and Eddie emerge with two boxes. "Got them," Bryan announces.

"Any vampires down there?" I ask.

"Nope, all clear. There's one more. I'll get it." Bryan places his box on the center island and heads back. I'm glad I didn't have to go back down there, but I'm not going to tell him that.

"Where do you want this one?" Eddie asks. I point to the floor, next to the island.

"Thanks, Eddie."

He nods and heads toward the bar.

"Eddie?" I raise my hand. He turns back around. "I'm sorry about the jokes."

He nods. "Doesn't bother me none. Bryan is more sensitive, I guess. He's had a hard time dealing with things these last few years." He leaves before I can ask him what Bryan had a hard time dealing with.

"I can sense that," Faith says. "He's always so solemn when he comes in every night. Seriously, he's not a happy man."

"I know," I say.

Bryan appears at the door of the basement. "You know what?"

"Nothing," I say, shaking my head. "Let's open these boxes."

Bryan places the last box on the floor and leaves the kitchen to join Eddie. Faith takes the one Eddie placed on the floor. I open the one on the counter.

"Pictures, I have picture albums and loose pictures," Faith says, rummaging through her box.

"You were such a cute toddler. Seriously, adorable."

"Focus, Faith. Not what we are looking for…I think." I peek in mine and find newspaper clippings and articles, and printed-out research papers on…astronomy of some kind. I didn't know Grandpa was into that stuff. "I'm not quite sure what I have in here. It's a bunch of articles and stuff."

Faith moves on to the third box and opens it, while I peruse the articles… stuff on solar and lunar eclipses, planet alignment, and stargazing. "This is weird."

"This is weirder." Faith holds up three black composition books. "He kept journals."

I grab them, pushing the articles back into the box. Faith takes the box I was looking in and searches it.

The journals are numbered "1," "2," and "3," and dated, with the first dated a few days after my birthday. I open that one and sit on the cold tile floor.

I flip through the journals. They all begin the same—addressed to me.

Dear Ellie,

I buried your father today. It was a small affair; few people came. After everyone left, I stayed at his gravestone and cried. He was my only child; a parent should never have to bury his child. I'm only glad your grandmother passed a few years ago and didn't have to witness this. It would have torn her heart out.

The sun was about to set and Lily, your mother, came out of the woods with you in her arms. Her face was soaked with tears, so I knew she loved your father very much. She placed you in my arms and you looked so peaceful. I don't think your father got a chance to hold you.

She told me I needed to take you and raise you. She said she couldn't handle things by herself and didn't want to hurt anyone else. I thought she was too distraught and didn't mean what she said. I agreed to take you for a while until she got back on her feet; maybe she needed time to get a job and save some money. I knew it wasn't going to be easy being a single parent.

I asked her your name, but she hadn't given you one yet. I asked if I could name you. I told her I'd name you after your grandmother, Genevieve Eleanor Whitaker, but I'd call you Ellie. She agreed that was a great name for you. She kissed you goodbye and left through the woods.

So, here you are in my little apartment above the bar, sleeping silently in the bassinet I made for you before you were born. You are so beautiful and I love you so much. I promise I'll be here for you. You're all I've got left, Ellie.

Love, Grandpa

"What's it say?"

Tears roll down my cheeks.

"Ellie, I think your grandpa knew about the eclipse and the planet alignment. That's all he had been studying by the looks of this box." She holds up a few articles clipped together in her hands.

"It's his journal. He kept a journal for me. But, he did lie to me. I thought my parents died together, but that's not what he wrote to me." I grab the three journals and stand. "I think I need to be alone for a little while. I'm going to take these upstairs." I rub the tears away.

Faith nods. "Okay. I'll be down here. I'll help Eddie." She brushes the dust from her pants and follows me out the kitchen door.

My little bar was no longer empty ; it seems like every coal miner had walked through the door. They all hush simultaneously and turn toward us. The only sound that can be heard is the squeaky swinging kitchen door.

Bryan stands next to his dad, Mitch. There is a whole pack in my bar; some I've never seen. All their aura's are similar. The rugged looking strangers, however, have a darker tint to their auras...a more natural earth tone. Eddie and Mitch's look more civilized somehow.

"Um..." There I go again, at a loss for words. What does one say to a pack of wild werewolves?

Mitch walks over and holds out his hand. I shake it. "Thank you for allowing us to use the bar to gather. Things are chaotic outside. We'll only be here a moment."

I nod and look at Bryan, who shrugs. Everyone stands motionless, staring at me, as if waiting for an important speech. It's uncomfortable. Even on the busiest of nights, when there are many more patrons, I don't feel like this...like they are all watching my every move. I need to get out of here.

"You're welcome," I say slowly. "Eddie, can you get them what they need?" He nods. "Okay, I'll...I have to go upstairs now. I'll be back later."

Faith puts on her apron. I head toward my apartment, but in the hall I bump into Shawn as he exits the restroom. "Oh, sorry."

He looks at me, not with his usual disdain, but with a more questionable expression. "No, I'm sorry. I didn't see you. I'm Shawn, by the way." He smiles.

Did he introduce himself to me?

"Yeah, I know. We went to school together. You've been coming to my bar for the past few years," I remind him. "I'm Ellie. Ellie Whitaker...the one that brings you beer each time you come in." Maybe I sound a little sarcastic, but he deserves it.

"Oh, right," Shawn nods, but seems a bit confused. "Well, good to see you." He shakes his head, as if he's trying to shake his memories free.

I nod, go into my apartment and lock the door behind me. Obviously, I've entered the *Twilight Zone*, or perhaps some alternate universe where people actually talk to me. I shake my head and climb the stairs, journals safely tucked to my chest. "This can't be happening. I must be dreaming...one long dream."

My mind is overwhelmed. I grab my grandmother's woven blanket from the couch, wrap myself into it. I skip to Grandpa's last journal and read his final entry. That's what I always do when reading a book: I hop straight to the end to see what happens.

Dear Ellie,

I've lied to you your entire life. I hope you can forgive me. I did so to protect you and being your only parental figure, I'm sure I made mistakes. I should have told you the truth before you left for college, but I was afraid you wouldn't go then and I know how much you wanted to go.

I'm dying of cancer and I'm afraid I don't have much longer. I didn't have the heart to tell you. There's no use in you suffering along with me. I hid it well these last few years. I thank God every day I survived to see you grow up into a beautiful young woman.

When I was diagnosed a few years ago, I was so afraid I'd die before you were an adult and they would put you into foster care. I couldn't have that. By now, since you are reading this, you know that The Event is coming and you'll have time to prepare for it. I've been tracking it for years; that's why the will has that stipulation in it for you to stay here. It's your only chance to go home.

I know you've never been happy here in Saint's Grove, and although you didn't know the reason, I did. You don't belong here. I learned the truth soon after I found out I had cancer. It's time you knew it too, Ellie.

I'm not sure I should be the one to convey this to you, so I'll let your mother tell you. Find your mother. She'll tell you what you need to know. She's alive, Ellie. She's living in the same cabin your father built so many years ago. He built it for Lily since she loved the mountain so much. I'm sure you remember the stories of the mountaintop and how your parents treasured it so.

Please forgive me, Ellie. I love you so much and I'm so proud of you.

Grandpa

Tears steadily flow down my face. My mother's alive—at least she was five years ago.

Chapter Six
Day One

The sun sets and the orangest of glows circles the treetops. A fall breeze rushes through and the trees tremble from the pressure, allowing slices of vibrant lights to seep through. Soon, the lightning bugs will appear and contribute to the festival of color.

As I stand at the window overlooking the woods, I realize that never before have I taken the time to appreciate all the wonderful colors these woods have to offer. Grandfather only ever heard my complaints about the solemnness found within the confines of this town. I regret not telling him about the good things I saw, or rather I regret not noticing them in the first place.

After reading through the journals, I realize Grandpa meant well by lying, or that he felt he was making the right decision for me to cause less pain. In truth, my mother abandoned me. For whatever reason, she still chose to leave me. I wonder how different my life would have been had I been with my mother. Is it possible she is still in these woods, high on the mountaintop? Does she think about me? When Grandpa went to her a few years before his death, she still refused, stating she wasn't capable. According to Grandpa, she acted erratic, irrational and a bit crazy.

I suppose living secluded in the mountains would make someone a little crazy.

Why didn't she want me?

It's been hours since I left the strange bar full of werewolves. I need to go down and tell Faith what I've discovered. After thinking it through, I know what I need to do, but I don't want to do it alone. I'm hoping she will help me. She has to help me.

My nerves are on edge as I descend the stairs. I listen for sounds from the bar, and pray I don't walk into what seems to be another silent film where I'm the star once again. As I get to the bathroom hall, I still don't hear a peep out of the other room. Maybe they have all gone. Mitch did say they wouldn't be long, right? At least, I think that's what he said.

I breathe deeply and crack the door open. I walk in when I see there's not a bar full of people.

Most of the wild-looking wolves are gone. Only a handful sit in the bar. Mitch, Shawn, Eddie, and a woman sit in Mitch's usual corner, empty glasses before the three men. The woman, a milky beauty with long messy black hair and dark brown eyes that match the earthly color of her aura, sits listening to Mitch. She's so thin. She's different from the other wolves surrounding her, that much I can tell.

Bryan sits in his usual corner, looking out the window. It seems normal, yet so much stranger than before. He doesn't look my way.

Mitch rises. The others follow suit. I walk toward the bar, where Faith stands behind it drying off some glasses. She looks up when she notices me and half-smiles. "How are you?" she asks, concern in her voice.

I nod. I'm at a loss for words, not sure what I want to say or how I'll ask for help.

"Celestria, thanks for your help, as always. We will stand guard in town tonight and rally in the morning," Mitch says. She nods. He hugs her. It's not a short friendly hug, but a hug that's more personal.

"Stay safe." She looks at each of them, then eyes me near the bar. She tilts her head, studying me, her eyes turning yellow for the briefest of moments. She runs to the door, quickly taking off.

Mitch and Shawn follow Eddie to the bar. I go around it so I'm facing them, standing next to Faith.

"What's happened?" I whisper.

"Ms. Ellie, thank you again for allowing us to use your bar," Mitch says, taking out his wallet. He throws a few hundreds down onto the counter. "You and your friend should probably take off for a week. Get out of town."

"Thank you for your concern, but I have reason to stay," I say. "Faith and I are going up the northern mountain to search for someone."

"We are?" Faith asks. Her eyes bulge, waiting for my answer.

Eddie, Mitch, and Shawn stare at me, all tired, looking like they haven't slept for a week. "It's too dangerous out there, Ellie. You have no idea what's in those woods now." Eddie shakes his head. "No, I can't let you. Your grandfather would kill me."

"Grandpa's dead, Eddie, so I doubt he'd kill you, although it seems anything is possible these days. I need to go up there though and no one will stop me—us." I nudge Faith.

"Absolutely." She nods. "I can take care of her."

"You're kidding right?" Bryan jumps from his chair to join in on the wolfy objections.

"Listen, gentle…wolves, I've been prisoner in this bar for the past five years. I finally found a possible way out of this shithole, so I'm going to do everything in my power to figure out what that possibility is, and *no one* is stopping me." I hand the bills to Faith to put in the register.

"Wait, why don't we compromise," Shawn says. "She wants to go up the mountain. I can escort her through the territory better than anyone."

Bryan exhales loudly. I can't make out what he mumbles.

Shawn glares at him. "It's not like you want any part of this, Bryan. You made it perfectly clear you weren't patrolling or helping us protect our territory."

The air feels thick between them. "You've never lifted a finger to help anyone other than yourself." Bryan roughly slides his chair in. "I'm leaving. Do what you want." Bryan glances briefly at me as he leaves the door, following a stare toward Eddie.

"Mitch?" Shawn asks.

Mitch nods. "I wish you wouldn't do this, Miss, but if you must, Shawn is a good guide."

"We leave at first light." Shawn tips his baseball cap. "See you bright and early." He walks out the door.

"Eddie, you lock up. You're staying here tonight." Mitch nods and leaves. It wasn't a question; more like an order.

"So, we're having a sleepover?" I ask confused, having been secluded in my room the entire day reading the journals, while plans took place downstairs in the bar.

"I'm staying tonight." Eddie latches the bar door and shuts it the best he can. "You girls sleep upstairs. I'll sleep down here."

"In the bar? It doesn't look comfortable," Faith says.

"If you could give me a blanket that would be great." Eddie raises his eyebrow.

"I can do that, but you have to tell me what's going on with the wolves," I say. "They're different and some I've never seen before."

"Yeah, what's up with the crazy-looking ones? I swear I wanted to wash that chick's hair. It was so knotted, and not in a cool dreadlocks look, either," Faith says.

"Their auras are different from yours," I say to Eddie.

"Auras?" Faith asks.

"Yeah, you're violet and Eddie is a chestnut

brown, like Mitch, Bryan, and Shawn, but that girl, Celestria…she's a darker brown, like the color of her eyes," I say.

"Since when could you read auras?" Faith asks. "I can't even read auras and I'm a witch."

"Since last night, unfortunately. It happened soon after the lunar eclipse," I say.

We both look at Eddie at the same time.

"We are a bit different," he says. "But before I go into that, you both need to make me a promise. Right here. Right now."

"Okay, what exactly are we promising?" I ask.

"You need to keep quiet about what you are," Eddie says. "You being a witch," he points to Faith, "and you being…whatever you are. Bryan called it right though. You aren't only human."

"Oh Jesus!" I know he is somewhat right. There's no denying something's off with me. After reading the journals, I realize Grandpa believed that as well.

"Why do we have to keep quiet?" Faith asks.

"Some of the pack want to rid the entire territory of others, thinking them all evil beings out for blood here in this realm," Eddie says. "Like your new friend, Shawn, for instance. He'd kill every witch he could get his hands on. He thinks they're all evil."

Faith harrumphs. "I'm not evil."

"I know that." Eddie rubs her arm. "Promise me you will both keep quiet and not do any hocus pocus around Shawn, all right?"

"What about Bryan?" I ask. "He already knows what we are."

Eddie nods. "He's the one who asked me to tell you to keep your secrets silent."

"Okay. No hocus pocus," I say. We both stare at Faith. I want to ask about Bryan and why he left saying he wouldn't help. He cared for me last night and then today, it's back to his cool, lonely self again. It aches in my chest that he left me…us in the lurch.

"Fine," Faith agrees.

"Thank you," Eddie says.

"Now, will you tell us about the wolves?" I ask, sitting on a barstool. Faith plops down next to me.

"Where do I begin? Legend has it this same type of event occurred more than 300 years ago, before Peter Saint settled here. Several creatures from different realms entered this town; it was a bloodbath. Last night was nothing compared to that awful fight, or so I've heard. My ancestors, half man/half wolf, came through. After the battle lasted over the seven-day window, our pack was stuck on this side of the portal, never to return home again."

"So werewolves settled in the town?" I ask.

He nods. "The pack stayed in this territory. We are territorial creatures. A few may have strayed through the years, but the majority remained. Even I left for a while, joining the Navy to see the world, but my nature lead me back. This is where I feel most comfortable."

"Is that why Bryan is unhappy? He feels stuck here?" I ask, curious as to why Bryan seems so miserable.

"Bryan tried to get away. He had a hard time accepting what he is. It's why he rebels, not following pack orders, and keeping his distance from the others, but he still came back." Eddie shrugs.

"Why is that woman Celestria's aura so different from yours?"

He smiles. "I was born here, fifty years ago. My parents were both in the pack as well. Their parents were before them, too. Our family tree goes back far, but not all of my family members were pack blood. Some of the original wolves mated with humans." Eddie sighs. "Celestria, and the others with that same color aura as you call it, are different. You don't recognize them because they prefer to live in their animalistic state mostly. They are all part of the original pack that came over the first time. They are immortal. We are not."

Faith and I look at each other. Her mouth hangs open. Just when I thought things couldn't get any stranger, we learn immortal werewolves walk the Earth. At this moment, I think reality is more absurd than fiction.

Chapter Seven
Day Two

It's 2:45AM. I can no longer sleep. Faith turns over, facing the wall. I sneak out of bed. Grandpa's journal entries plague my mind. His love for me makes me ache for him so much more. I wish I could reassure him that I forgive him. He was always there for me growing up. I respect him even more for that now.

The journals contain information I wouldn't want anyone else to read so I hide them in the only place I think they will be safe—the air vent. Since I won't be bringing them on my journey, I feel better knowing they will be out of reading view of anyone that may break into my little home.

Turning on my fake fireplace on the TV stand, I sit on the couch watching the red false flames shoot upward. Grandpa couldn't install a real fireplace, due to the cost and location of the kitchen downstairs, so he bought me a fake one several Christmases back. It even makes crackling noises. Curling up in my grandma's blanket on the couch, I stare into the red wavy paper until I can no longer keep my eyes open.

"It's time." Faith shakes me.

"What?" I sit up. I must have dozed. The sun has already risen. The light penetrates the apartment. "Oh."

"The wolf is here…downstairs. Eddie knocked on the door and you didn't budge. Must have been tired," Faith says. She walks to my kitchen area. "I made you some tea." She fills my large bottle with ice and pours the hot tea into it. The ice melts quickly, but it doesn't take much liquid to fill the container.

"Thanks." I get up and stretch. "I must have dozed off when I came to sit on the couch." The fireplace had been turned off, probably by Faith. "What time is it?"

"Eight. We should get going. Walking up that mountain will take all day. Vehicles don't fit on the trail from the base. We'll be hiking it most of the way." She hands me my tea and grabs a filled backpack.

"You're prepared."

She nods, holding out my tennis shoes. "You can't hike barefooted." She's dressed in jeans and a hoodie over a t-shirt. I don't think I've ever seen her in jeans. She looks so tame and normal.

"Give me a minute to get ready." I take the tennis shoes and head to my room.

"I'll be downstairs," she says.

The unsweetened tea tastes so good. Grandpa

always made fun of me drinking unsweetened tea. He said it wasn't southern of me. "We only drink the sweet stuff here," he'd always say.

"Maybe I'll start drinking the strong stuff later," I'd say. I smile and change into jeans and a sweatshirt.

Eddie and Shawn sit at a table with no beers in front of them—a sure sign the world is definitely upside down. Faith stands at the window, peering out into the square. "We should probably leave around back." She turns toward me, her backpack on.

I nod, taking another swig of my tea.

"Yep, that's best," Shawn says, watching me as he grabs his backpack from the chair. "Too many people around in the square this morning."

"What's in the packs?" I ask.

"Necessities." Shawn pats his pack. "Water, blanket, matches...things like that."

Faith nods. "We need to go. It'll be a long hike."

"We aren't taking a car to the base?" I ask.

Shawn shakes his head. "I couldn't get my truck through town. We'll have to walk it."

"Let's go then," I head through the kitchen to the back door. "Eddie, are you staying?"

He nods. "I'll take care of the bar and maybe help around town if need be." He follows us to the door. "I'll make sure it's safe. Don't ya worry none."

"I'm more worried about you." I hug him goodbye.

"Shawn, take care of my girls or you'll have to deal with me." Eddie winks at me as Faith pounces on him for her hug.

"Will do." Shawn leads us down the back alley street, north, straight toward the mountain.

The click of the lock sounds comforting. At least he'll be safe.

The alley stands quiet, but the noise from the town square drifts over the rooftops. My eyes search the woods in back; for some reason, they seem different. They aren't the same woods I played in when I was younger. These woods hold secrets…secrets that are dangerous and foreboding.

Faith watches the woods, too. We walk in silence for a long time, until we are safely out of town and have entered the russet forest floor. Fall has turned a lot of the leaves different colors and many have fallen, covering the earth with vibrant, wet hues.

"Aren't we taking the path?" I ask. The path is about a half-mile west of where Shawn leads us.

"This is faster," he says. "It's more crowded with trees, but we'll save some time."

He slows until I catch up to him. Faith follows a few feet behind. "Okay."

"What exactly are we looking for?" he asks.

"There's a cabin at the top that belonged to my parents. Have you ever been there?" I ask. Surely his pack have every inch of these woods mapped out, having been here for centuries.

"Actually, this is my first time going to the top. That's not a part of our territory. I was told it belonged to the mountain woman and we were not permitted there. I'm kind of excited to see what's up there…and with such pretty company, too. I guess this bloody event brought some good things about after all." He winks and my stomach churns. He was such a bully in middle and high school.

The wind sweeps through, causing the leaves to rustle and bringing a shiver down my spine. Birds chirp up high. I see a red bird perched on a branch. Our feet sound so loud in the forest, as if we are disrupting the silence it requires.

"Why do you need to see the mountain woman anyway? Rumor is, she's not right in the head," Shawn says.

"She might have answers about my mother." I trip over a covered up tree trunk. Shawn grabs onto my sweatshirt, making it constrict against my neck. He pulls me back up.

"Be careful." He rubs my back.

"I'm fine; thanks." I pull away and right myself. "Why didn't you go away to college? Or join the military after school?" Faith steps between us.

He walks forward. "Didn't have the mind to do either, I suppose. Besides, Bryan ditched us and his father took me under his wing. The pack has to stay together, but Bryan didn't see things that way. How is it I can't remember you from high school?" He looks at me.

"I was there. Maybe you were too busy with your own group to notice anyone else," I snap too harshly.

"I would have noticed you." He winks. It's unnerving to witness. "I admit I was selfish back then, being kids and all. Isn't everyone at that age?"

"I wasn't." Faith purses her lips.

"I suppose," I say.

Our climb quickly turns uphill. Shawn is there every moment, helping me with my footing. He can't keep his hands to himself, but he doesn't help Faith the same way. Something is off with me now, and it's driving me crazy.

We've walked for hours and the sun beats down through the trees directly overhead. My stomach growls. I swear it echoes through the forest so loudly, I blush. I forgot to eat breakfast and my body argues with me.

"I've got it covered!" Faith smiles. She holds up her backpack. "It's time to eat."

She pulls out a blanket and covers the damp leaves. She made sandwiches for us; all peanut butter and jelly, but they hit the spot. My calves ache and I'm glad for the rest, so I eat the sandwich slowly.

"What do you like to do in your free time, Ellie?" Shawn turns toward me, his back to Faith. She rolls her eyes.

"I, um, read a lot," I say. "But mostly I run the bar."

"That's boring," he says. "I should take you out sometime to Roanoke. Get you away from town for a while. It'll be fun."

He chomps down on his sandwich, taking half of it in one bite.

"I rarely get time to go anywhere," I say, but I'm hoping I won't be around here much longer at all. Shawn may be a cute guy, but he's so stuck on himself it's not funny. He hasn't even called Faith by her name once.

"Are there more?" He turns toward her. She pulls out another and hands it to him.

"Werewolves," Faith mutters. "That's your dinner, too, you know."

"Hey, we have big appetites." He shrugs, chomping into his second sandwich. There's a jelly smear on the corner of his mouth, but I don't want to point it out to him. "We should get going soon. Don't want to be stuck out here in the dark," he says, with the bite still in his mouth.

Maybe werewolves don't have great table manners. I think of Bryan, but I've never seen him eat, so I can't compare.

I nod. "I need to go to the bathroom first." I look to Faith. "Come with me?"

She rises from the blanket and clears the crumbs from her jeans. "Let's go."

"Don't wander too far," Shawn says. "I'll head in that direction. I've gotta go, too." He gets up. "Scream if you need me." He winks and takes off west.

Faith and I head east, far enough away where we can't see hide nor hair of Shawn.

"Thank god! I needed to get away from that creep," Faith says. "He's so macho…arrogant and downright rude."

I giggle. "He means well."

"He means to get into your pants is what he means," Faith says. "It seems all the males are drawn to you lately. Don't think I haven't noticed."

"It's not my fault," I say, but wonder if that's the truth.

We squat and take care of our business so quickly, it's funny. I guess neither of us want to bare our bottoms longer than necessary. It's a bit chilly out.

"I hate using leaves," Faith says.

We stand near a large tree and laugh at ourselves. "You have to admit, this is hilarious. Us, out here in the woods, with a werewolf as a protector?"

"I don't need a damn protector. He's a moron."

"Be quiet. He can probably hear you."

"So?" She smiles, and the strangest thing happens.

All of the sounds in the forest cease.

"Faith, do you hear that?"

"Hear what?" She turns. "I don't hear anything."

"Exactly."

That's when a small shadow emerges 20 feet away. A small creature steps into view.

"What the—?" Faith instinctively steps back.

It's a little girl. She's pale white and bows her head so her long blonde hair hangs to her waist. She can't be more than four or five years old. She wears a long dress that seems excessively big. That's when two more shadows emerge to stand next to her –two boys the same height as her, both with blond hair, too, only theirs hangs to their shoulders. They are dressed in dirty shorts and plain black t-shirts.

I realize it's not shadows I'm seeing—it's their

auras. They're black. These kids' auras are black. At that moment, all three look up. Faith gasps. Their eyes are solid white. These kids aren't kids at all.

Chapter Eight
Day Two

The little girl opens her mouth. It's a big black, gaping abyss filling half of her face. There's no tongue, only a massive void, but then the sound of ear-piercing windy static penetrates my ears and knocks me backwards onto the ground.

It's as if a tornado whirls through my head. "Faith!" I scream. She stands between the weird kids and me. She holds up her hands and recites something but all I can hear is the loud whirling wind.

A black cloud forms above the children, bearing down on us. I scream louder than I've ever screamed. If Shawn can't hear that then he won't have anyone left to lead up the mountain. These demon kids have to be from Hell. Is Hell another dimension that leaked its inhabitants into our world? Lord help us.

His faint howl sounds so distant. He's not going to make it in time.

But then, the whirling tornado in my head slows. The black cloud crumbles to the leafy ground...it looks like falling black ice. I sit up and watch the kids, one by one, turn to solid ice. Their faces freeze. The large abysses of dark nothingness that are their mouths remain frozen beneath a sheet of ice.

"Faith?" I ask, but she stands erect, still facing them and continuing to mouth inaudible words.

The gray wolf appears behind me, growling, as Faith finishes freezing the little turds. Faith turns and the gray wolf jumps at her becoming a streak of blurry fur.

Faith turns sideways to blunt the attack, and he clamps down on her like a rabid dog.

"No!" I rise and jump onto his back, which surprises him. We tumble into the leaves. My back hits a tree trunk, but he lets go of Faith, who now lies on the ground, bleeding.

The wolf shakes before me, vibrating my entire body, and Shawn appears next to me, naked. I push him away, and he's on his feet faster than lightning.

"Faith!" I yell.

Shawn stands between us and blocks me from her. "She's a witch, Ellie." The disdain in his voice is apparent. "She'll kill both of us."

"No, she won't," I say adamantly, as tears escape my eyes. I can't hold them back. Faith holds the side of her stomach, and her eyes seem desperate.

He growls, and the sound is awful coming from his human mouth. "She needs to die. She won't live out the day, anyway. I need to put her out." He steps toward her, and my mind races with confusion.

I want to scream; anger boils inside me and then

there's something more I want now…

"Shawn?" I say in a voice I never knew I had. I'm practically singing his name so seductively it's scary. I touch his naked, sweaty shoulder and nudge him to turn toward me.

His eyes gloss over instantly as he peers into mine, almost as if he's under my spell.

I smile seductively, wondering where all this sensual energy had come from. "Come closer and give me a kiss."

This strange, new ability of mine both scares and empowers me. I don't have time to consider it. I need to save Faith.

He tilts his head ever so slightly, and I feel the pull of his chestnut aura drawing me in. His lips part and his aura pulses faster. Our lips touch and a spark sends a shiver through me. I hold his head to me and allow his sensual aura to flow through me. He grabs my waist and attempts to push me away, but my grip tightens and I feel strong—his energy makes me stronger.

His eyes widen and his cheeks become pale as his aura dims little by little.

The euphoric pleasure fills every inch of my body and I want every last drop Shawn has to offer. I feel the life slipping from him and entering me—and I want more, so much more. His hands go limp and fall to his side. His chestnut aura disappears and I release him. His body drops to the ground.

"Ellie?" Faith watches me, surprise lighting up her face. "Your eyes…"

Energy pulses through me and I feel like a shining beacon beckoning ships to shore.

"Ellie?" Faith lowers her voice. She still holds her stomach, and I see blood dripping from her wound.

"Oh God, Faith." I try to shake off the sensation of this stimulating pleasure that roams through my head, but it's useless. I kneel beside her and assess the situation. "Does it hurt?"

"Nah! It stings…a lot, like a thousand jellyfish stung me at once. Yes, it hurts, damn it! Help me up."

Lifting her up feels easier than I thought. Faith winces. "Sorry," I say. "We need to get you some help, fast."

"Get it," Faith takes a deep breath and coughs. "The bag." She points to her backpack.

Holding her up, I swoop it up with my free hand and fling it on my back.

"Should we get Shawn's, too?" I ask.

She nods, and we head toward where we had picnicked not long ago. I take one glance back at Shawn's withered body lying on the damp leaves. Guilt rears its nasty presence for the briefest of moments. I did that. I took his life. Panic washed through me, clenching my chest. Sweat beads on my brow, despite the fall air. Jesus. I killed someone, and I liked it. Yes, Shawn had been a jerk, but in my right mind, I never would have considered murdering him…with a kiss.

I couldn't think about it, though. We needed to keep moving. I push the thoughts aside and concentrate on putting one foot in front of the other.

Hiking this mountain with Faith injured isn't going to be easy. It'll be slow-going from here on. My mind races thinking of how to find help in the fastest possible way. I have no medical training and I don't know how to help Faith.

Shawn's bag sits perched against the tree trunk. I grab it, swinging it over my shoulder with the other bag. It's heavier than Faith's pack.

"Water." Faith licks her cracked lips. I set her down carefully on the ground and reach into her pack for a bottle. She sips it slowly. "Thanks."

I nod. "Are we closer to the top or the bottom?" I look north and south. I can't figure it out.

"I think we're closer to the top." Faith coughs, the water spilling from her lips.

"Careful. Do you think we should go *up* for help?"

She nods.

"Maybe we shouldn't talk too much?"

She nods again. I help her to her feet. She leans into me and we continue our trek upward. This mountain-woman had better have an emergency phone or medical training, or Faith's in trouble.

Hours pass. It seems we haven't gotten far. Faith leans into me harder than I expect and I almost tumble over.

"Sorry," she says.

The fireflies appear and dance around us. It's becoming harder to see ahead as the shadow of darkness envelops us under the canopy of trees.

"Ellie, we should stop." Faith places her hands on

the next tree we pass. "I don't think I can walk anymore."

"Okay." I drop the packs onto the ground next to her. "Let me get the blanket out."

I sit her on the corner of the blanket and wrap the rest around her. "What about you?" she asks.

I shake my head. "Don't worry about me. Maybe Shawn has one in his pack, but right now I need to start a fire. The temperature is dropping fast."

Searching the woods nearby for dry wood becomes difficult. I gather as many twigs as possible, but most are damp. I have to go further away from Faith to find better pieces, and the woods creep me out. They become a blanket of blackness, which causes the hairs on the nape of my neck to stand up.

Faith watches me build a little teepee from the sticks, with a few large pieces in the middle.

"Aren't you the little Girl Scout."

"Hardly." I open Shawn's pack. "He said he had matches, didn't he?"

She shrugs.

He has a change of clothes, which I lay on the ground. He has several bottles of water, a knife, a box of matches, and I pull out what was weighing the bag down…a gun.

"Oh Jesus!" Faith coughs again. I think he bit into her lung.

"That's not a hunting gun."

"I don't think werewolves need hunting guns."

"There's no damn blanket. I guess werewolves don't need blankets, either."

I light the fire with dried leaves. The twigs catch fire, thank goodness.

"That's better," Faith says. "Want to share my blanket?"

"No, I'm okay," I lie.

I move toward her and open her blanket to check on her bite. "He got you good, didn't he?"

"Damn dog!" she mutters and laughs, which turns into a fit of coughing and wheezing.

I take the extra shirt Shawn brought and press it against her wound. "Ouch!" She slaps me away.

"Sorry. I was trying to help."

"By causing me more pain? Thanks." She closes the blanket, keeping the shirt underneath against her bite. "Camping sucks, by the way. It's not nearly as much fun as I imagined it. We don't even have any marshmallows to roast."

I laugh. "Do you ever take anything seriously, Faith? Here we are, fending off evil entities from God knows where, and you're still cracking jokes."

She smiles. "There's no changing who I am. So, do you want to talk about it?"

"Talk about what?" I ask, but I know what she means.

"Oh, I don't know...about killing a guy?"

I shrug. "I didn't know...I mean, I had to do something and..." I shrug again, and sit next to her near the fire.

"You didn't know what you were doing, did you?"

"My instincts took over and it happened."

She smiles. "You sounded different. Like a singing siren calling him to his death. It was utterly bizarre."

"Not as bizarre as freezing a bunch of little kids," I remind her. "Is that all you can do?"

She nods. "That's what I'm best at. I mostly ignored my mom's teaching. Honestly, I didn't want to be a witch. I went through the motions, but I loved the ice-freezing spell. It reminded me of Elsa's power in *Frozen*. That was one of my favorite movies."

I giggle.

"Hey, I was young, okay?" She smiles and coughs again.

I grin. Even in the throes of pain, she still has her sense of humor.

"Ellie?"

"Yes?" I poke the fire with a long stick.

"I don't want to be a werewolf." Her mouth frowns at one corner.

"You're not going to be a werewolf," I reassure her. "You'd be more of a were-witch."

"That's not funny."

"I'm teasing. I don't think a bite from a werewolf turns you. You heard Eddie. They were all born into it."

She nods. "I hope you're right."

The crackling fire mesmerizes me. I watch the flames dance in the air. We hear the howling of a wolf, and we both look at each other.

In the distance, we hear bushes rustling and footfalls in the leaves. I grab the gun and scoot closer to Faith.

"We haven't eaten dinner, yet," Faith whispers. "I don't want to die on an empty stomach."

"Shh." I aim the gun in the direction the sound is coming and pray it isn't a vampire or demon of some kind. I tremble as the intruder nears our camp. I've never shot a gun before, but there's always a first time for everything, right?

Chapter Nine
Day Two

My palms sweat as I hold the pistol. I try to aim straight, but my trembling fingers make the barrel point in different directions. The footfalls against the leaves become louder with each passing second. Faith and I remain silent, but the crackling of the fire gives us away. Anyone would be able to find us in the dark; I was stupid to think we could pass through the night unnoticed with a blaring fire signaling every creature in the woods to our location.

The vampire I saw during that first night pops into my head. He attacked so quickly and with such callous disregard…not to mention the other creatures that have crossed our path during this strange time. It seems so many monsters want to hurt and kill, without understanding the other species they face. Well, some of them need what the other has—the blood running through our veins, or the life energy that I sucked from Shawn.

Am I different from any of them?

The feet are right on top of us, and the gun slips from my sweaty hands, but not before I pull the trigger, firing high into the treetops.

Faith flinches, closes her eyes and covers her ears. I reach for the gun, as our intruder appear in the light of the fire.

"Whoa!" Bryan holds up his arms and drops a backpack onto the dirt. "No more shooting there, okay?"

A brown wolf emerges behind him, violently shakes and reveals his human form—Eddie. A naked Eddie stands before us.

"Oh, that's not right," Faith says and covers her eyes.

"Eddie! Do you know how much you guys scared the living crap out of us?" I put my head between my knees for a moment to try to slow my heart beating.

"Do you know how much you scared us?" Bryan asks. "One of the pack found Shawn's body in the woods and alerted the others."

"Faith, you're hurt." Eddie bends down next to her. "I smell blood."

Faith starts crying…uncontrollably.

"Eddie, put some pants on." I throw him Shawn's leftover sweatpants. He puts them on in record time.

"What the hell happened?" Bryan unzips his bag and pulls out bandages and a bottle of something I can't make out.

"It's all right, Faith." Eddie picks her up and holds her in his arms like a baby. "Shhh." He rocks her, and slowly takes off her cover to reveal the wound.

"Tell…tell me I won't become a werewolf," she sobs through the tears. She winces when Bryan applies the liquid from the bottle.

"Shawn bit her," I say.

They look at each other. Bryan wraps up her wound.

"No, you won't be a werewolf," Eddie reassures her.

She breaks into a coughing fit, with her tears flowing. I've never seen her this distressed. Today's events seem to be catching up with us, and an emotional wall threatens to break down inside me.

"She needs a doctor," Bryan says. "The wound will heal, but I think she's got fluid in her lung since she's coughing like that."

Eddie nods.

"We were going for help, but we didn't make it far." Tears stream down my face. I'm afraid I'm about to lose it, too. Faith's strength kept me strong and now…I'm weakening.

Eddie stands with Faith in his arms. "I'll take her." Faith winces and moans.

Bryan nods.

"Now? In the dark?" I ask.

"No, you stay here. I'll be faster without anyone with me," Eddie explains. "We'll be okay, Ellie; don't worry."

Faith looks at me and sniffles. "You find your mother, Ellie."

"What?" The concept seems so distant now. "No,

I want to be with you."

She shakes her head. "You need to find her and learn about *you*."

Thoughts of killing Shawn linger.

I nod reluctantly. "Okay, but I'm coming back down tomorrow." I look at Bryan. "Will you help me?"

I wonder if he's going to take off with them, but I'm hoping he'll stay with me. I don't think I'd survive the night.

"I'm here to help you." His mouth twists.

"Be safe." Eddie looks at us. "And put out that damn fire."

Bryan stomps on it and a few embers remain lit. Smoke billows in the air.

Eddie runs into the forest with Faith in his arms.

"They'll be okay," Bryan wraps his arms around me. "Eddie is faster than any of us."

His embrace warms me. The moonlight is now our only light in the darkness, and the noisy bugs become our only company. An owl hoots in the distance and continues his boisterous cries for what seems like forever. Owls may be considered regal and magnificent birds, but I'd throw a rock at that one right now if I could.

"Here." Bryan holds out a new blanket he must have plucked from his bag. I sit in the damp leaves and allow him to wrap it around me. He sits close. I can feel the smallest amount of heat releasing from him.

"Why no fire?" I ask, but I'm certain I know the

answer. It was what I was thinking moments before they arrived. I'm fishing for conversation to ease the night noises from my mind.

"Attracts attention," he says. "What happened? We found Shawn's body and those freaking frozen white-eyed kids and assumed the worst."

"Uhh, well, those kids attacked us, or were going to, and Faith froze them to save us, but Shawn bit her, and said he was going to kill her 'cause she's a witch, so I killed him," I say, within the span of 10 seconds flat, looking away from him toward the darkness to the east.

"You killed Shawn? You, sweet Ellie who wouldn't move away when being stalked by a vampire?" Sarcasm fills his voice. "Exactly how did you kill Shawn?"

"I know he was your best friend, so I'm sorry about that, but he was going to kill her. I didn't have a choice." I apologize, changing the subject as best I can. It's not easy to explain the how of the situation.

"He was my friend a long time ago, but I'm not mourning his passing. You don't need to apologize to me, but I don't think we should tell anyone else you did that. Let them believe those wicked kids did it, okay?"

I nod.

"Now, how did you kill Shawn?"

I shrug. "I'm not entirely sure, but I think I kind of sucked the life out of him."

"Well, one doesn't hear that every day."

"Why did you leave the bar last night? You left

and didn't help us or anything," I turn toward him, but I can't make out his expression in the dim light. I can't help but resent him at this moment; had he been here instead of Shawn, I wouldn't have taken his life...at least I don't think I would have.

"I, um…" He stumbles over an answer.

"You, um what?" I turn toward him and give him an evil glare, but I don't think he sees.

"It didn't look like you needed me anymore, so I left. Shawn was going to take good care of you. I did come by in the morning and watch you leave through the back of the store though."

"You did? Were you jealous of Shawn?"

"Do you know why I come into the bar every night?" He faces me. We are inches apart.

"To get a beer after a long day."

"No. I come to your bar because you give me hope. I've hated what I am for so long, and I despise my job, but for the last two months I see you working and running the bar every day, without fail. You have no family left, but you persevere. You don't talk about anyone in town negatively, and you live alone. I've never once seen you go on a date, but you wake each morning and do it all over again." He shrugs. "I figured if you can do it for one more day, then so can I."

"Is that true?" It's the sweetest thing anyone has ever said to me, and all of my frustration evaporates into thin air.

"It's the truth." He raises his hand and places it on the side of my face. I lean into it and close my eyes.

His warm touch feels so good against my skin.

The thought slams into me like a brick. What if it's my new alluring power that draws him to me, and not what he said?

"Wait." I pull back. "Shawn and everyone else look at me differently now, like I'm some kind of Aphrodite. What if I have that power over you, too? It isn't fair that I draw you in like that. It isn't fair to any man."

He shakes his head. "I noticed the difference that night, right after the portals showed up. You grabbed your head like you were in agony one moment, and then you rose and appeared so majestic."

"See, that's it. You're only attracted to me because of what I've become."

"No, that's not it Ellie. I was already attracted to you. When you changed, I knew I had to protect you. I knew your world was about to be turned upside down, and I couldn't stand the thought of not seeing your smiling face once a day."

He leans into me and slowly brings his lips to mine. Excitement builds up in the core of my body, but I have no temptation to squash out his life aura. A new fiery feeling awakens inside, and I fall back against the leaves as our kiss deepens. His hands move to my face and gently roll down my cheek to the back of my neck. This is the sensual kiss in romantic movies that I always imagined but never experienced.

His mouth parts from mine and moves down my neck. His gentle caresses send tingles down my spine and awaken a burning need I haven't felt in so long. A soft moan escapes my lips as he moves his hand down the side of my body. Heat rises to the surface and the coolness of the air no longer matters. His warmth is all I need to survive this night.

The gentle chirps of the morning birds awaken me before the light penetrates the treetops. Bryan's naked body presses against mine, his arms wrapped gently around me. I don't want to get up. I want to stay in this moment forever. It feels so right…so comfortable.

I blink the sleepiness away from my eyes, only to see the barrel of a shotgun pointed at us.

Chapter Ten
Day Three

Elbowing Bryan was not an ideal wake up call, but I didn't want to say anything. He grunts, "Hey, I didn't think you'd be the sleep hitter type." He kisses the back of my neck.

I clear my throat loudly, my gaze still on the gun and the shadowy, hooded figure holding it on us.

"Huh?" he asks, and I assume he sees the danger since he jolts up and climbs over me, putting himself between me and the gun. He holds his hands out. "Whoa, we aren't here to harm anyone."

"You're in my territory," a woman's rough voice speaks from under the hoodie. "You don't belong here. We made a deal."

She looks left, then right, and back to us. Her motions are fidgety, and she's clearly looking for other intruders.

"We're searching for someone, that's all." Bryan's calm voice impresses me. I'm sure I'd be a blubbering mess if I could talk.

"I don't care who you're looking for. They sure as heck aren't around here." She looks left and right again, and Bryan turns his head each direction, as well. "Were you followed? There're strange things in the woods lately."

Bryan shakes his head. "No, Ma'am."

"Good. Well, get on out of here." She points her gun toward the woods, motioning us to follow it. "You wolves stay away from here." How did she know Bryan was a wolf, and what made her think I was one, too?

Bryan wraps the blanket around me, exposing himself to the bare morning air and the strange woman holding us at gunpoint. He grabs his pants and quickly pulls them up, then hands me my jeans. I turn from the lady and shield myself from her crazy, darting eyes that look like marbles.

"Come on now, get." Her restless hands jerk the gun. "We don't have all day."

"We're moving." Bryan hands me my shirt. He packs up the blanket and closes his pack, flinging it over his shoulder.

I face her, our eyes lock, and I'm able to get a better look at her. "Mountain Woman Brickell?" I recognize her rugged demeanor. She's not tall, perhaps shorter than my 5'7" if she'd stand up straight. Her face looks worn, no doubt by her age and hermit living.

"Aww, damn!" She stares at me. She lowers her gun until the barrel touches the ground. "You're from the town…the bar gal." Her visits to town are rare, but the locals know her by name. She's never once come into the bar, but does, on occasion, go to McHale's Grocery. Some folks even say she frequents the cemetery, but she always keeps to herself.

"You were there the other night. I saw you on the grass." Then, I look for her aura. It's not there. I can't see it. I turn to Bryan and his is still chestnut brown.

The Mountain Woman nods. "I ran, like everyone else. I ran back to my mountain. And I'm not going back. Too many things came through, most not good."

"Your mountain?" I probably should have spent time looking at the appraiser's site to see who owned the land.

She nods, parts her lips and closes them quickly.

"My parents had a cabin on this mountain, long ago. I was told that at least five years ago my mother still lived there. Do you know where it is?" I point north, tall trees blocking the path.

The strange hermit watches me for what seems like a minute, then shakes her head. "You should leave. I can't help you."

"She needs your help," Bryan pleads. "You know her mother, don't you?" He narrows his eyes.

She shakes her head and again peers to the left, then the right. "Damn it! Go already!" She pauses for 10 seconds, and shakes her head, looking like she's arguing with herself. "Damn it to Hell! I can't let you leave these woods yet. I spotted a demon about a half mile away from you before I left the house. Let's get out of here. It's safer at my place and out of these damned spooked woods." She takes a deep breath and leads us up through the mountain of trees.

Bryan and I glance at each other. He slowly moves his head side to side, pursing his lips. He thinks she's lost it. It makes me think about her lonely life up here and how she deals with the solitude. We all need people around, don't we?

The morning birds greet us as we move along, their songs waking each other from their rest. The leaves crumble under our feet, making our steps louder in our silence. The mountain woman glances in several directions along the way, as if she's watching out for things she doesn't want to find in the woods, and I want to know what she's seen. "What strange things have you seen in the woods lately? What did the demon look like?" She doesn't mask her anxiousness well.

"I've seen fairies and demons. The one I saw nearby was tall, brown, and had several spiked horns protruding from his head. Doesn't look like a pleasant fellow."

"Fairies?" The strangeness doesn't cease to amaze me.

She nods.

"We saw demons, too, I think. It was terrifying. How did you get away without them attacking you?" I ask, curious if she needed to use her shotgun. Can a shotgun even hurt a demon? Those little devil children we encountered probably couldn't be killed by a shotgun. Had Faith not been there, I'm sure I'd be dead.

"I saw them. They didn't see me."

"What did the fairies look like?" Had this woman said this to me mere days ago, I would have thought she was nuts—and who knows, maybe she is. Grandpa used to tell me fairies lived in these woods, but I never believed him—until now. "Have the fairies always lived here?"

"Nasty little creatures." She shakes her head. "They can be little or big and creepy. Whatever they choose."

Not a good description, to say the least. My imagination runs wild, picturing them as scary, sharp-toothed winged beings depicted in nightmarish tales. "Did you know about fairies?" I ask Bryan.

He shakes his head and rolls his eyes upward, indicating she may have a few screws loose upstairs.

Brickell continues to move her head around, facing too many different directions, I'm sure she's going to get whiplash. Perhaps if she took her hood off she'd see better.

The path steepens and Bryan pulls me up in a few places, until we clear the trees and enter into a green pasture. Mountain Woman Brickell has no trouble making her way through the dense forest. The aroma of wet grass greets us, and I breathe in deeply. A cabin sits on the far side of the green hill and relief floods me that we don't have to go much further.

It's the only cabin I see, and I know we are at the top of the mountain. We can see for miles in all directions; clouds cover the treetops like a winter blanket. I look south and see the town, but it looks so much smaller from up here. A clear path breaks at the south of the meadow, heading down the mountain toward the cemetery—at least I think it would lead in that direction. How did we make it this far in such a short time? It feels like it should have taken us days to arrive.

"This was my parents' cabin, wasn't it?" I ask, making my way toward the wooden porch. Plants hang from hooks, some with a few blooms left in them. A rocking chair sits in the corner of the porch and I want to rest in it, but the inside has piqued my interest.

"It was," she says, and my stomach drops. She said it in the past tense, and now I wonder if my mother lives at all.

"Did you know her?"

She nods. "A long time ago." She looks off in the distance, perhaps recalling a far off memory of my mother. "Things are much different now."

"How is that?"

She opens her wooden door, and it creaks as it moves inward. "For one, I'm getting more visitors these days. I'll have to move further into the woods to keep away from people."

"I'm not so sure people are the problem." Bryan points to the edge of the meadow and three scantily-clad women in white dance toward the tree line. Their laugh carries on the wind, along with a scent of lavender.

"Damn nymphs!" Brickell raises her shotgun, but

Bryan places his hand on the barrel.

"I don't think shooting them is the answer."

"Damn nuisance is what they are. All they do is dance all day long, and sometimes in my garden. Not once do they contribute, either, but they'll help themselves to my vegetables. Damn lazy creatures."

I laugh. "I think that's the first creature I've seen that didn't try to kill us."

They caper around for a few moments, their pink auras shining bright in the morning light. We watch them disappear into the trees. Morning dew covers the grass and I see the allure the meadow has. It does look magical; however, I don't see any little fairies flying about. It's kind of disappointing.

"Let's get inside." Brickell ushers us into the cabin. She glances around again before latching the door with a long wooden log that sits in the cradle on both sides of the door.

It hits me as I look around. My parents lived here, I was born here. Grandpa said I was born in the cabin. After reading his journals, it was the same day that Dad died. My birthday will never feel the same again. He wrote my father died of heart troubles he knew nothing about. Guilt rises to the surface; maybe my birth stressed him too much...being alone on this mountain with no medical team to help might have been traumatic.

The cabin is as Grandpa had described many times to me growing up—a fireplace in the middle of the main room, facing the south, with a rug covering the wood floor in front of a feathery couch. The front door faces east. There's a kitchen area with antique looking appliances and a wood burning stove. A small pantry contains tons of self-canned vegetables; Brickell's been busy readying for winter. A wooden table with four matching chairs rests near the stove. Stairs lead to the loft below the triangle shaped roof. Windows in the loft face both the east and the west so the sun greets them in the morning, the sun leaves them in the evening, making way for the stars to shine bright for them in the night.

It looks exactly as I imagined it when I was younger. It's so fairytale-like. It's clean, not as I expected with the mountain woman living here. I rather pegged her for a packrat with junk piled high in the corners or animal skins and traps scattered about, but that's not it at all. She's taken care of it. A tear rolls down my face as I think about how happy my parents must have been here.

A few framed pictures sit on the mantel over the fireplace, and I step forward to see them. One is of my parents standing in front of the cabin, it's old, but still holds a hint of color. They are both smiling. The picture next to it is of a baby in a cradle—my cradle—the cradle Grandpa made for me. On the far side of the mantel is a more recent picture; it's me graduating high school.

I point to it and see the expression on Brickell's face.

"Are you my mother?" She looks nothing like the woman in the picture, but why else would she have these pictures here on her mantel? Maybe she's an aunt I never knew existed. Confusion grows by the moment and I need answers.

She breathes out, removes her hood, undoes her cloak, and places it on the couch. That's when I see her. Her skin clears into a smooth whiteness; her wrinkles disappear before our eyes; her hair shines with a deep black and her eyes glisten with a soft emerald luster, which complements her soft green aura. It's as if she had emerged from the Fountain of Youth. That's the woman in the picture on the mantelpiece next to my father.

"Yes, I'm your mother. I wish you hadn't come to find me, but I understand your reasons."

Chapter Eleven
Day Three

The light drifting in through the windows seems to dim under her softly glowing aura, and my knees feel weak. "I need to sit," I say. Bryan helps me to the feathery couch. He takes a water from his pack, opens it, and hands it to me. "Thanks."

He nods. "Sip slowly."

"I'm sorry, Ellie." A crease forms on my mother's brow.

What is she sorry for? It could be a number of things, I think, as each pops into my head. Is she sorry for abandoning me when I was an infant? Is she sorry for hiding from me in seclusion all these years? Is she sorry she tried to push us away in the woods and didn't want to help us?

An anger builds inside me, and it's not an emotion I was expecting to feel at this moment. To be honest, I never expected this moment to come. A part of me wanted her to be dead.

My tears fall. "What are you sorry for, exactly?"

"I'm going to go outside and leave you two alone." Bryan kisses me on the forehead and heads toward the door.

"Wait," my mother says. "Take these and be on the lookout." She hands him a pair of binoculars that were hanging next to the fireplace. He takes them, looks at me once more, then leaves the cabin.

His hiking boots give away his presence as he moves around the front porch, heading in the direction of the rocking chair. If I can hear him, I'm sure he can hear what's happening in here. The cabin isn't exactly soundproof.

I wipe away my tears and sit straighter on the couch.

My mother sits next to me, after latching the door. "I'm sorry that you had to kill someone." She raises her hand to my face, as if she wants to brush away a falling strand of hair, but pulls it back without touching me.

"Kill someone?" Then Shawn comes to mind.

"Your aura is a darker shade of green, almost the color of a crocodile that's been lurking in the muck. Green is our color, you know, the color of life and healing."

A thousand questions form in my mind. "Our color? What am I...I mean, what are we? Where do we come from? What's wrong with me?"

"Shh..." She gently takes my hands into hers, resting on my lap. "I'll tell you everything you want to know, but slow down. I haven't spoken to many people in a long time."

She looks out the window toward the west. "The closest thing that's described in Old English folklore is a succubus. In this world we don't exist, but we have a world of our own, as do all the creatures that arrived through the portals. Some come from far off lands, some from the past, and maybe even from the future. We lived in a different plane of existence, and when the portal opened between our worlds, our curiosity brought us to your world...I mean this world."

"I'm not human." The word echoes in my head. *Succubus.*

She shakes her head and frowns. "I was hoping you would be like your father—human. I didn't think it was possible you'd take after me." Her gaze meets mine. "You can see other people's colors, can't you?"

I nod.

"What colors have you seen?"

"Lilac, brown, pink, and black. Oh, and yellow." I'd forgotten about Drunk Richard. His was yellow.

"Lilac is a good shade for a witch, but be wary of the darker shades. Always be wary of darker shades," she says. "Purple means magic. Brown for the wolf, symbolizes nature. Pink—I imagine you mean the nymphs—symbolizes love, and black—"

"Evil," I interrupt.

"Yes, unfortunately. All colors have meaning in this world, and it's our way of seeing the type of person—I mean being—they truly are."

Her hands give me comfort and warmth. I can't stay mad at her, seeing how beautiful and peaceful she is with me at this moment.

"Ever since the…event the other night everyone looks at me differently. Before they never saw me and now they won't stop noticing me," I say. "I sucked the life out of Shawn—a wolf. He attacked my friend." A shiver runs through me as I say it aloud, and the scene plays over in my head.

"We have a natural allure about us, but you can learn to control it," she says, not further remarking on the news that I killed someone. "You need to practice with meditation and calm. The more anxious you become, the more difficult it is to control."

I shake my head, trying to free the thoughts loose.

"What about that cloak?" I shift focus to another question weighing on my mind. "That hid your appearance."

"It's a magical cloak and I paid a great price for it. It's helped hide me all these years, but seeing you in the woods, having your aura shine out like that—I knew my solitude was nearing an end. I honestly thought you were safe from all of this. When you went away to college, I thought your life was normal and you'd find happiness. I didn't expect you to come back to town, and I certainly didn't expect you to turn."

"Things become more bizarre as the days pass." I lean back into the fluffiness and feel the wood against my neck, thinking about the life draining from Shawn into me. This memory will never escape me. "Did you take lives where you're from? Did you even have humans in that plane or whatever it's called?"

She shakes her head. "We didn't need to take human life. There were none there to take. We lived off the sun's rays or the energy in the earth. It was our sustenance. But, here, things are different. Your sun is not as bright and the biggest beacons of energy happen to be humans. I soon learned that taking a human life allowed me to live longer."

Every time she answers one question, another 10 pop into my head. The sheer thought overwhelms me. "Do you take lives here?" I wonder if Mom is a murderer, hiding in the mountains.

"I haven't taken a life in a long time. I don't want to have to do that, and I've aged because of it. I don't have your youth any longer." Her hand sweeps down my face and she smiles.

"You look beautiful though. Not a day over thirty, which is way too young to be my mother, by the way."

"We age at a slower pace."

"Was your name Lily in the other world?"

She nods. "No one has called me that in many years. Your grandfather was the last to call me that. He knew I live here, hidden beneath my cloak."

I think I'm suffering from information overload and my questions jumble around in my head like a disorganized puzzle so it's hard to prioritize them. I need a moment to think.

"I, um, I need some fresh air. Do you mind?" I point toward the front door.

She nods and leads me to the door. "I'll make us lunch." She opens the door for me to leave. "Don't wander in the woods though, please." I nod.

The grassy meadow looks so vibrant. I take a deep breath and rest my body against the railing, facing the meadow. The rocking chair teeters on the wood. I see Bryan smiling at me. He tries to be reassuring, I know, but I don't think anything would have prepared me for this lesson.

"These binoculars are fantastic, but no demon sightings," Bryan says, looking through the lenses toward the south. "I never thought I'd say that in my life."

I laugh.

"How's it going? Kind of intense, huh?"

"Yeah, kind of overwhelming and intense." I move closer to him.

He pats his knee and I join him in the rocker. "But, you found what you were looking for, didn't you?"

I cradle my head into his chest. "Yep. I guess."

"But?"

"But, I'm not sure I was looking for these answers, and it's so different than what I truly expected. I'm confused, and I don't know what to ask or how to say what I'm thinking."

He wraps his arms around me. "Breathe. Close your eyes, take in the fresh air, and listen to the sounds of nature."

I do as he says. The bugs in the meadow sing their sweet songs along with the birds of the forest; even the sounds of their wings flap in the air. The wind sweeps the treetops, whistling through the leaves. The sounds could put me to sleep.

A few moments later, he breaks my reverie. "Now, is your mind clear?"

"Mm hmm," I say.

"Think about the question you most want to ask your mother. Take your time, and try to put all the other nasty events out of your head."

He kisses me on the top of my head and rocks me back and forth. He smells of wood and trees, and fresh cotton. The thought of his lips first touching mine pop into my head, and I relive that one sweet moment we shared last night—this isn't helping me concentrate too well at all.

"Lunch is ready," my mother calls from the door. "I'm afraid I don't have much to offer, but fresh vegetable soup is on the menu. I don't get to town too often."

Reluctantly, I rise from my comfortable spot and stretch. "Give me a sec," I say to Bryan as he passes me to go into the cabin.

Seeing the leaves wrestle with the wind brings a calm about me, and I think of my mother's words when she was telling me I can control the alluring side effect to my condition. One day, I'm a working human intent on leaving town and taking control of my destiny, and the next I'm a succubus trying to control my urges to suck the life out of people.

Grandpa was smart. He knew I was different and tried to protect me the best way he knew possible— he lied to me. I used to think lying was a weakness, but I've learned lately it's also a virtue. My mom lied to me, too. She hid the truth from me. She hid herself from me, and in that, she was a lie. Could it be her lies were for honorable reasons, as well?

Here I am, able to get the truth, and I think that scares me most. The one question I want to ask her, and that I want the truth to, suddenly becomes clear. I take a deep breath, turn toward the door, and walk inside to ask it before I lose my nerve.

"Mother...Lily...Mom—" I'm not sure what sounds comfortable to me, yet. "There's one question I need to know the answer to right this moment."

She sits and waits for it. Bryan scoops a bowl of soup from the wood stove, and the aroma makes my mouth water, but I can't let it deter me from my current path.

"Why did you abandon me? Why did you leave me with Grandpa?" I ask not one, but two questions that are basically the same.

She sighs, breathes in, closes her eyes, and holds her breath for a long moment before releasing. "I didn't want you to get hurt."

"What do you mean?" I walk closer to her and kneel before her on the chair. "What do you mean you didn't want me to get hurt?"

"I was afraid I'd do the same thing to you that I did to your father, and I couldn't bear the thought of losing you, too." A tear escapes her eye. "You see, he gave his life to save both of us."

Chapter Twelve
Day Three

'*H*e gave his life to save both of us'. I repeat the words over in my head to try to grasp their meaning and I shudder.

"I'll, um, eat on the porch," Bryan says. Guilt builds inside me that he has to witness our reunion. I couldn't have made it here without him, and I'm entirely grateful, but I know it's not the most comfortable situation for him. He walks to the door, bowl in hand. "It's good soup, by the way."

"Thank you." My mother gives him a half-smile.

Once he's gone, we sit in silence. The bowl of soup stops steaming on the table before her and she doesn't touch it. I allow her to gather her thoughts. She looks as if she's figuring out the best way to start her explanation.

"I hadn't always stayed in this town, you know," she begins. "After the bloody war that proceeded once we entered through the portal, many of our kind were murdered. I guess all our kind, with the exception of me. We weren't a strong species, not trained in war and fighting. We come from a loving, peaceful place. I was so young then, merely ten years old; a part of the royal dynasty that ruled Asteria. It was a bright place, with sunshine blasting us all but a few hours each day—not like it is here. Our home moved more slowly around our sun and our habitat stayed in its rays the majority of our year. We were closer to the sun. At least, that's how I remember it. It's been so long that I think sometimes I don't remember things right."

She shakes her head, and continues. "I'm going off track. Anyway, it's in the past, and can't be changed. It was pure chaos at the time we came here, and the details get blurry when I try to remember all that occurred. My mother perished quickly, and when my father realized what was happening, he grabbed me and ran, but he wasn't fast enough. A blade pierced his back and he fell, tumbling over me in the process. He told me to run and hide, and get as far away as possible. That's what I did.

"I ran for so long, scared and alone, not knowing what had happened to the rest of my family. Eventually, I couldn't carry on in these mountains. I cursed them a thousand times over in that moment. Days later, a native family found me curled up in a bush, starving for nourishment and thirsty for water." She moves toward the window, looking out to the west. "They raised me with their children and taught me how to love the earth and nature and what it had to offer. As I grew older my body started to crave more energy. One spring day, while picking blackberries with one of my adopted sisters, we were captured by a neighboring tribe. Fear triggered my power. I seduced them easily and took their lives. There were five men. My sister witnessed this. I sent her home and never returned to the family who was too kind to me."

She stands in silence for a minute. "I traveled the world after that, once I became more acclimated to the people. I learned my powers could prolong my life here. I hunted for the worst human offenders I could find when I needed to feed, but I became tired having lived so long. I returned here twenty-five years ago, when I gathered my nerve to try to find out what happened all those years past." She shrugs. "I guess I was hoping to find someone from my world who made it through the massacre, or maybe a way to get home. All I heard were superstitious rumors and folklore the townspeople didn't know to be true, but then I started noticing that not everyone in this town was human. I could see their colors, but they didn't know I was more than human. I could live amongst them, feeling a little comfort in our differences from the humans, but I never expected to fall in love."

She turns back to me. "I met Junior, your father, on a trail in the woods. The woods were where I felt most at ease, and we had that in common. There was so much goodness in him, and I could see that with his bright yellow aura. He had bought the mountain and desired to build his home here, away from the town, surrounded by the nature and forest he loved so much. His dad had helped him with the money, in exchange for the promise he would help with the bar. Your grandfather treated me like his own daughter and welcomed me warmly. Your dad and I were married two years after we met. After we finished building the cabin, he insisted we have a place to make it official, and start a family."

She walks to the mantel and looks at the picture of them together in front of the cabin. "He even accepted the truth when I told him about me and where I came from." She laughs. "He didn't doubt the truth of it one little bit. I thought he would have me locked up, but he rather loved asking me questions about the past, about my home, about the things I've seen and where I've been. We always had something to talk about."

She pauses and comes toward me, bending down in front of me. "I didn't think a pregnancy was possible for me." She shakes her head and a few tears trickle onto my knee. I didn't wipe them away. "You grew inside of me and I grew to love you. Your father was so proud and excited we were going to be a family. He always said you would be a girl, but by the time you arrived..."

She places her head on my knees. "When the time came, something was wrong. I was bleeding too much and becoming weak—too weak. Your father didn't have time to go down the mountain to fetch the doctor. I knew I was dying, and I knew you were withering away inside, too. He begged me not to leave him. He couldn't live in a world I wasn't a part of."

Tears steadily stream down her cheeks. "He put his lips to mine and told me to take him with us…and I did, I took his life. His energy flowed through us and I pushed—and you came crying into this world. Your father lay dead next to us. My happiness and sadness all within a few moments of each other. His energy provided us life. Looking at you next to him made me vow, at that moment, I'd never again take another life. I would live out my days as a human, and I had to make sure I could never be tempted to harm another person I love…and that only person is you."

"So, you gave me to Grandpa and stayed away from us both?"

She nods. "That was the only way I could assure you would be safe from me." She rises and sits next to me on the couch. "Can you forgive me?"

I nod. "It seems you and Grandpa lived lies to protect me."

"I've been alone ever since that time, and I've suffered greatly, feeling the best part of me was so out of my reach. There hasn't been a day that has gone by I don't think about you, or try to glimpse you in my binoculars. Even seeing you take the trash out brings me joy, and when I realized it was you on my mountain this morning, well, I panicked. I've only wanted you to be safe and all I have ever known is you're safe away from me—but then the portals opened..." She gets up, eager to do something. She pushes the bowl of soup in front of me. "Are you hungry? You must be. You haven't eaten all day, and evening will approach soon enough."

"I am going to get Bryan." Her words play over in my head, and I know she's sincere. I truly believe she has suffered and my anger subsides.

He sits in the rocking chair, the empty bowl on the railing.

"I'm so sorry," I say. "I didn't think this would be one long roller coaster ride along the way."

"Shh, come here," he says, and I sit in his lap. "I've enjoyed being with you, and I'm happy you're finding the answers you need."

"I've enjoyed being with you, too."

He brings his lips to mine and kisses me softly, and then more deeply. Butterflies flutter in my stomach and a sense of joy rises to the surface. I feel exactly why my parents were happy here in this place. It's peaceful, beautiful, and secluded.

My stomach growls. He pulls back. "You need to eat." He chuckles at the roar of my stomach lion. "And I need to eat more, too."

"You're right about that." We go inside and grab Mom's vegetable soup. It is the most delicious soup I've ever eaten. I guess fresh mountain gardening is the secret.

Mom starts a small fire, telling us we shouldn't have it too big or it may attract unwanted attention with a large smoke stack billowing out of the chimney. We sit and talk for hours. She asks me about school, the town, and the bar. I tell her about Grandpa's will and how he requested I stay in town for this alignment of the planets and the lunar eclipse.

I tell her about the journals and answer everything she asks…even the trivial questions like my favorite color, the yellow of the daffodils in the spring; or my favorite types of books, horror and thrillers, although I'm liking horror a bit less these days. In telling her all these things, Bryan gets a glimpse into me, too.

The evening shadow of the setting sun turns into darkness, with moonlight shining through the windows in the loft, making it seem like it glows inside.

"And how long have you two been together?" She stares at Bryan holding my hand as we sit on the rug in front of the fireplace.

Heat rises into my face, probably making me look like a ripe tomato.

"We've grown up together, but I was such an ass for too long that we didn't know each other well until recently," Bryan says. "For the past two months, since I've been back from college, I've seen her every day." He smiles at me and squeezes my hand. "If it weren't for her, I'd have gone crazy by now."

"Took you long enough to say something," I tease.

"If you both want to take the loft, I can sleep on the couch tonight," my mother offers. "The couch is comfy enough for me, I'm worn out."

"Thank you, Lily." Bryan calls her by the name she asked him to earlier. He stands and stretches. "We'll take you up on that offer." He pulls me up off the rug and hugs me. We climb to the loft and lay our heads down on soft feathery pillows. We opt for laying on top of the quilts for now, but I suspect I'll be climbing underneath after a while. Cool air seeps through the windowsills above and brings a chill with it, along with a crisp fall smell of damp leaves.

The stars shine brightly in the sky and I imagine my parents spent countless hours staring at them and talking about the past and the future, about where they've been and where they'd go, not knowing their time together would be cut short. This truly is one of the best features of the entire cabin. My father knew exactly how to build the perfect home, and the even more perfect sleeping area.

"It's amazing up there, isn't it?" my mother asks.

"Beyond," I say.

"Don't spend too much time awake staring at the stars. We need to leave first thing in the morning."

I turn and look down toward the couch, seeing her smile at me. "What do you mean leave? We only got here." Tonight was so great, I want more nights like this—with Mom and Bryan, getting to know them both, walking in the woods, tending to her garden, and listening to her stories of the past, all that she's seen. I haven't even scratched the surface of what I want to know about my mother, and then I think about the bar and Faith. Being up here almost made me forget all of the important stuff—my friends. More guilt forms in the pit of my stomach. What if Faith didn't survive the bite?

"Well, if my calculations are correct, then those portals will be closing in four days, on Halloween," she says.

"Your calculations?" My mind swarms with mixed thoughts of Faith, Eddie, and the strange happenings in our town.

She nods. "According to the old stories that circulate in these parts by some of the creatures that arrived when I did, the portal will close after seven days."

"Shouldn't we stay away from all that? Wouldn't we be safer up here until it's all over?" I ask. The horrid creatures I've encountered pop into my head.

"It might be safer, but then we would miss our chance."

"What chance?" I ask, oblivious to her meaning.

"Our one chance to go home, Ellie. Home to Asteria—to our kind."

Chapter Thirteen
Day Four

Asteria—is it another planet far away, in an alternate universe? Bryan sleeps next to me, Mom rests on the couch, and I'm wide-awake. The stars shine bright above and all I can ponder about is the strange place my mother comes from. Is it possible to return?

Four days. Perhaps we can make a quick trip there to see if we like it. We...I watch Bryan sleep next to me and contemplate—*we*. His perfect complexion should be a sin. This entire experience is surreal. How did we get to this point? Would he venture through the portal with me? Is it even permitted? A thousand questions pop into my head that I don't know the answers to. I could have kept Mom up all night asking her things I want to know.

A wolf howls in the forest. Bryan twitches, but doesn't wake. It makes me wonder if it's Eddie or one of the others. Are they trying to communicate with Bryan? Should I wake him? I choose not to, allowing him to rest; he'll need strength for tomorrow.

There are millions of stars, or at least it seems that way…too many to count. If I'd paid more attention in astronomy maybe I could name the constellations.

My nerves won't allow me to sleep, so I start counting the stars from left to the right. I close my eyes and for a split second I see them on the inside of my eyelids. My sweet starry sky.

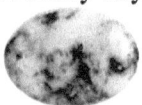

Kisses attack my face. My eyelids flutter open.

"Good morning." Bryan smiles at me. "Time to get going."

The sun hasn't risen fully, but Mom's feet shuffle across the wooden floor below letting me know that she's all ready to get moving down the mountain.

"It's so early," I say.

"We need to get moving so we aren't stuck in the woods after dark," Mom says. "Get on down here and eat some oranges."

"Oranges?" I climb down the loft stairs after Bryan. "You can't grow oranges here."

"I do go to the store from time to time, you know. McHale's Grocery…Brian trades me goods for some fresh vegetables from my garden."

"I wondered how you got by up here," I say. "I've seen you in town only a few times all these years. Must be incredibly lonely."

She shrugs. "I've been around a long time, so I have my ways."

We eat our oranges. Mom packs a few more for the road, puts her cloak on, and grabs her finely engraved walking stick. Her appearance changes and her aura disappears, an amazing sight to witness. Bryan grabs his bag. We head out into the fresh mountain air.

The birds flap about, squawking at us, as if telling us to stay clear of the ominous woods. The sun is high enough to make the forest appear more inviting, but I'm still cautious. Demons don't only come out in the dark, at least not the ones we dealt with on the way up the mountain.

"Do vampires only come out at night?" I ask, remembering the pale skin and the sharp teeth of the one I witnessed up close. "I mean, that's the old folklore, but since I didn't believe they existed before, I'm not sure what is or isn't true about them."

"The ones who came through the last time were nocturnal visitors, and those are the ones I'm sure most of the older stories are based on," Mom says. "Not all of them perished on this plane. Some learned to adapt to the environment, hiding in the shadows."

"Unbelievable." I turn toward Bryan. "Did you know about them?"

Bryan grabs my hand. This is the first time we've walked while holding hands, and it reminds me of how Mom and Dad met in the forest. I'm sure they walked hand-in-hand all throughout these woods.

He nods. "I've heard stories about them from time to time. At first I thought they were all nonsense, but then I pondered it after I came of age and began turning with the full moon. I figured if I existed, then vampires could be real."

"Do you turn at every full moon?" I ask.

He shakes his head. "The older I became, the more I was able to control the shifting. I learned how to calm myself and how to change when I wanted. It's that way with all of us—I think."

"Those others, the immortal ones, how are they different?" I ask.

He shrugs. "I'm not entirely sure. We never spent much time with them. They kept to themselves and roamed through the northern territory. Sometimes we'd go years without catching a glimpse of one. When the portals around town opened, they showed up."

"I don't think my mind is processing this all too well. Sometimes, I think I'm dreaming this entire event."

We hike a little further. Going down the mountain seems much easier than climbing it was. My calves ache still from the other day, but it's bearable.

The tall trees shade us from the sun's rays and I wonder about Asteria. Are there forests there? "Can you tell me about Asteria?" I ask Mom. "Is it similar to here with trees and snow and the changing of the seasons?"

Mom shakes her head. "It's different. We were close to the ocean. In our world, our people stayed in a tropical area, that is where we thrived. Time doesn't exist there as it does here. We did not measure our years or celebrate our birthdays. We lived in peace and all cared for one another." She pauses and breathes deeply. "It was so long ago and I was so young, full of days spent playing and being happy. Perhaps the politics are more complicated than I recall, but my parents always seemed at peace."

"Were there a lot of us, our kind?" I ask. The humans have one hell of a population problem in certain countries.

"Not like humans, Ellie," she laughs. "I guess you can say humans to us are like breeding bunnies. There are more than what the world can sustain. I do remember that when an elder passed, a new life existed. We were never sad or angry at the loss, but rejoiced with the changes. Our bodies seemed to co-exist with nature. It provided for us as we provided for it. That's the best way I can explain it." She shakes her head. "It's as if we were moving trees, connected to all other living things."

"You miss it," I say. Her eyes light up and a smile appears under her cloak.

"Very much. Would one not miss peace?"

"I suppose not."

Bryan peers ahead into the trees, his pensive stare searching for something I can't sense or see. Maybe I shouldn't talk about Asteria; he may not want to hear about it. Even though we've been around one another throughout our lives, we only connected a few days ago in a different manner. It's so new, but feels so old and comfortable.

"You'll love it," Mom says. "It's where we belong."

"What about…others there? There are no humans, but what about animals, or other creatures?" Bryan's wolfy form enters my head.

"We have animals of all kinds. Some not of this world. They are not kept in zoos or hunted. They co-exist with us. There are deer, and all the creatures of the forest, which is why I feel more at home in these woods than anywhere, I suppose. But, I always wondered if things escaped into our world as they escaped into this one. I'm not sure how our people would have handled demons, vampires or werewolves."

I nod. "Why did you choose to come here?"

"Like humans, we are curious, as are most kinds, I'm sure. When the portal opened, our healer convinced my parents it was a sign of a voyage we should partake in. The world wouldn't show us anything it didn't want us to do, of course. I guess we were a naive species, huh?"

"Naive? I don't think so. How could you know what was on the other side?" I ask.

"We were too trusting. My father insisted the royal family enter first and return to report our findings. It was a privilege, he felt, for us to move through the strange darkness before us. My father, holding me, was the last to enter, following my mother, aunt, uncles, and cousins. The healer was the first through. No one survived, of course. At least not that I can remember. I always hoped some of them were able to escape and make it home after witnessing the chaos and death that happened here, but it's unlikely."

"Maybe they did," I said.

"I suppose it's possible." She smiles. "What about your kind, Bryan? Where did they come from?"

"I don't think we have a story as miraculous as yours, Lily. We've only ever been told stories around the campfire. Our ancestors came through from a dying world to inhabit this one. Once they were through, chaos broke out and they were attacked by some devil-like creatures from Hell. Soon after, the portal closed and the survivors made their home here. Some left to live in other areas, and others remained close. After a while, a few of our kind fell in love with humans, and we are the product of those unions."

"Do you believe the story?" I ask, since he seems so matter of fact while telling it.

"I'm not sure. I want to ask one of the originals, but they keep their distance from us. That is, until this happened. Maybe my dad can get the real story now since we've united for this purpose." He squeezes my hand. "I do know several have perished throughout the years—killed by hunters or hit by cars."

"I'm so sorry."

"That's the way of the world, isn't it? They don't believe we exist, yet they're still driving us to extinction."

A strange anger exudes from him. Maybe he does resent his nature. Being only half-human, I can relate, but I've not had to endure the change he has. I squeeze his hand and smile.

Hours pass. We hurry down the mountain, skipping time to sit and eat, eating as we walk. The closer we get to the base of the mountain, the quieter we become.

"We're near the cemetery," mother's voice whispers on the wind, reaching our ears.

The sun races toward the western sky and my heart begins to beat faster. Could we be so lucky as to make it to the bar before the sun leaves us helpless? We successfully hiked down the woods with no sign of another creature, good or bad, along our way.

Bryan stops me from moving forward as the first of the gravestones come into sight. He lifts his head and breathes deeply, then shakes his head, pointing toward the graveyard. He smells something, or someone, near.

Perhaps our luck has run out. I turn west and see the sun sinking below the horizon, and my heart beats faster still. I feel it'll leap out of my chest at any moment.

We edge toward the cemetery gate that serves as a barrier between it and the forest and see people clustered to the north of the graveyard. They appear human, or humanlike; their heads seem a bit larger and their eyes further apart, but still human, if it weren't for one tiny detail. Their auras are blue—a bright cerulean blue.

Chapter Fourteen
Day Four

One of the figures, holding a silver device projecting 3-D holograms above it, points in our direction. The others turn and see us cowering in the trees. I try to hide behind a tree trunk, but they know we're here.

"It's okay, Ellie," Mom says. "Look at their auras."

"I see their auras, and they're not human. Aren't humans yellow?"

"Look again." She moves toward the fence between the woods and the cemetery.

Bryan holds my hand and brings me back around the tree so we are facing the strangers standing thirty feet from us at the far edge of the cemetery. Most stare back at us, while some huddle, working on their futuristic-looking devices. Their auras are a light color, and I recall Mom's lesson on the lighter colors being the friendlier of the creatures.

Bryan keeps his narrowed eyes on them as he helps me through the wooden fence into the graveyard. We need to pass through the cemetery to get to town, and Mom acts as if they aren't a threat.

The graveyard is spooky at dusk. The gravestones nearest us are older, while the more modern stones lay on the other side of the street, where my father, grandmother and grandfather are buried. I thought the gravestone next to my father was my mother's, but that was apparently a ruse. A tall oak grows in the center of the older section; I always admired the scenery when I'd come with Grandpa to visit. I hadn't been here in five years, so I'm sure their graves lie in disarray. The town mows the grass but it doesn't maintain the stones.

The strangers seem so out of place here among the old headstones and monuments. "What are they then?" I whisper to Mother.

She shrugs. "I've never seen them before, but I don't think they're evil."

"How can you be sure? The lighter color?"

She nods. "They aren't looking at us in a threatening manner. They are probably more afraid of us." She motions with her head toward the group. "The aura waves."

I watch the blue auras dance around them. They're nervous, I think, or at least their auras act that way. I nod at Mother. She taught me another thing about reading people I had not noticed before. Their actions and feelings affect their auras.

One of them steps away from the group, approaching us, acting as a buffer. He's pensive, yet nervous. "We are leaving." I don't recognize his accent. His voice shakes; perhaps as a warning or plea? He holds up his right hand and a shiny, silver bracelet blinks a white light across its surface. The gesture seems like a peace offering. He's telling us he does not pose a threat to us.

"We are, too," Bryan says, as he ushers me in the opposite direction. "We're not here for you."

The man looks relieved and nods.

I stop. On the other side of him, the others stand in front of something.

"Look, it's a portal." I point and walk toward it. The man backs up a step. I slow my advance. I didn't realize I had startled him.

Bryan pulls at my hand. I turn toward him. "I want to see it."

"We don't know what they are. Even Lily doesn't know."

"Then, we'll ask," I say, appearing more confident than I truly feel. "They're not threatening us."

"I guess curiosity runs in the family. Let's make this quick." She gazes at the setting sun.

"Great, crazy runs in the family." Bryan rolls his eyes.

I yank his hand and pull him to me. "Did you call me crazy?"

"No, well, maybe." He smiles, kisses me, and follows my mother.

The one with the silver bracelet who spoke to us, an older man dressed in a white button-down, short-sleeve top and khaki pants, speaks to one of the younger men and walks a few steps cautiously in our direction. He looks uneasy; his hands fidget and he looks back to the others in his group—five men and three women—and then back at us.

"You shouldn't be out much longer," the old man says. "The sun is about to go down and there have been some rather nasty characters out the last few nights. Even the majority of your town stays indoors after dark." He gestured in the direction of the town.

"We are heading there now." I look around him at the portal. "You are all leaving through there?"

"Where are you from?" Mother asks.

The man turns around. One of them nods.

"We are leaving in a moment, yes, to go back home."

"What are you?" I ask. "You're not human."

He stares at me. "And you aren't, either. And neither is the man you hold onto tightly, but you do have differences. The woman in the cloak hides who she is."

I purse my lips and squint. "How do you know this?"

He holds up his bracelet. "We are from a distant place where things are less hostile than Earth—and more advanced."

"Your bracelet tells you we aren't human?" I raise my eyebrows.

"Our bracelets tell us a lot of things. Without them, we wouldn't be communicating with you, as English isn't our language."

"Where are you from?" I ask the same question

my mother asked. She's right, I'm curious.

"Another time, another place, but we are close biologically to humans. You are a curious girl."

"You came through the portal, the same as all the other...things?" I ask.

He nods. "It was an opportunity to see this plane, this place, meet these people and determine if they are worthy of our assistance. It was a learning experience, as well as an opportunity for data collection."

"Now you're leaving? Did you find what you were looking for?"

"We found resistance, aggression, hate, and violence." A tear rolls down his chin. "We came with twenty and return with eight."

"Blue signifies peace," Mother says. "You're peaceful people."

He nods. "You see colors. We haven't encountered a kind like yours before. Evolution over centuries has brought us to a peaceful existence, but Earth is not nearly there. It is in a state of turmoil."

"I, too, come from a more peaceful place, but I haven't seen it in a long time," Mother says. "I understand your longing to go home."

"It's The Event. It's brought things here that aren't the norm for Earth," I say. "Half of the things you've seen aren't from here."

He shakes his head. "It wasn't The Event or the creatures—things that came through from different planes we were expecting. It was the humans we came here to study. We met with unfortunate circumstances along the way. Humans still have a long way to go before they learn from their mistakes. They still fight, battle in war, destroy the nurturing body that supplies substance and sustenance, and still see differences amongst them, not realizing we are all the same. We need to go now. Our place and time is ready to receive us."

He turns to look at the portal. His people hold out their hands with their silver bracelets before them and step through the portal, one at a time.

"Good luck to you," he says, facing his people.

"And to you," I say. He's given me a lot of spiritual heaviness to ponder. I feel sorry for humans, of which I was only days ago. He's right though—we do focus entirely too much on our differences. Bryan catches me staring at him.

We watch them step through the portal and disappear into another place, or perhaps another time. Part of me wants to think they were from the future, but I'm not so sure Earth has a future, if it keeps on the path in which it continues to make more mistakes.

"Mom, can we go to Asteria through there?" I step closer to the portal, but keeping my distance in case anything wants to come out. I envision a perfect existence full of love and peace awaiting our arrival.

She shakes her head.

"Why not?" I ask.

"If we step through that, at this moment, there's no guarantee where it'll take us."

"I'm so confused."

"It's an open doorway to many places. We need

the right key to get to Asteria and I only have half of it." She bangs her walking stick into the ground.

A howl erupts in the mountains, and Bryan watches the woods. "We need to go now. The sun is going down and we have a half-mile to get to town."

Chapter Fifteen
Day Four

"What the hell happened?"

No one answers me, and we run away from the cemetery, racing the sun to town. Once we hit town, we slow our pace. Bryan grabs my hand, keeping his eyes on everything around us. His brown aura waves become tense and uneasy, swaying in different directions.

The town appears quiet as we hurry down the street. A few people linger, and some crowd near the statue at the center. The general mood reeks of a somberness I've not felt before. Although I've never been particularly happy living here, others seemed to be. As I grew older, I noticed things like that about people and I felt utter envy they found happiness here.

We pass quickly by the closed bank and post office, and race past Bare Wook Furniture and the Sunshine Cafe. The things around me blur as I focus on getting back into the bar, but off in the distance, near the bookstore, I see a lone figure staring at us.

My uneasiness grows.

The bar door is locked.

Bryan pounds on it, and looks into the window. "Eddie's coming," he says. I turn to look at the bookstore again and the man standing there moves around the corner. I can't make out his aura this far away, but I'm sure he's observing us. I guess with all the craziness going on, everyone wants to know what's happening around town.

A couple of clicks and the door opens. Eddie reaches down, hugs me, and picks me up, twirling me in a tight circle.

"Good to see you, too," I say.

Mom comes in behind me and Bryan shuts the door, locking it back up.

"Where's Faith?" I look around the empty bar.

"I'm here." She pushes through the kitchen door, a blanket wrapped around her like a shawl. "It's about time you guys got back. We were worried sick."

I run to her and hug her.

"Ouch!" She backs away, holding her side.

"Oh, I'm sorry." I cup my mouth and nose. I'd forgotten about her bite.

"She refused to stay in the damned hospital," Eddie says. "She insisted on coming back here and waiting with me for you to return."

"You're okay?"

She nods. "It's a little sore. I'm happy I won't be a damned werewolf, though. That would have ruined my plans. They had to drain my lungs, but I'm ten times better now."

Faith gives my mother a puzzled stare.

"I, um, have a lot to tell you. Meet my mother, Lily."

Mom takes off her cloak, revealing her true self to Eddie and Faith. I think Faith's eyes are about to pop out of her head.

"Yeah, we have lots to talk about," Faith says. "Let's sit down."

"We're starving." I hold my stomach. "We didn't stop all day."

"Got it." Bryan heads to the kitchen. Eddie helps him, propping the kitchen door open so he can hear our harrowing tale of the last two days.

We eat, and for the first time ever, I can't seem to say enough. I tell Faith and Eddie everything that happened, from me being a succubus and seeing the nymphs in the woods to Mom holding a shotgun at us, and how she explained things—it seems I'm an awful storyteller, as I flip from one thing to another without going in chronological order. The only thing I left out was the alone time Bryan and I shared the night they left us. That's too special to tell anyone, and I hope that Bryan remembers it as fondly as I do.

Eddie's face remains brooding, while Faith seems shocked. They listen without interrupting. Eddie refills our beers a few times and my mind becomes woozy with the last round.

"I'm rambling on. I'm sorry. What's happened around here?"

"Eddie took me straight to the hospital. It was a

madhouse in there. They've been trying to keep up with the people that kept coming in. I didn't want to stay another minute and be in the way. They're more than doubling up in the rooms. It's crazy, but somehow they're managing to help everyone."

"She made me take her out," Eddie says. "She was going to leave with or without me."

"She's stubborn like that. What about around town?"

Faith shrugs. "I spent most of yesterday upstairs recuperating. Mom read me a healing spell that worked wonders. Eddie's been running the bar, but he's being selective on who comes in. We're closing up before dark, like a lot of the places in town."

"Healing spell?" I shake my head. "You have to teach me that one someday."

"What about the undesirables?" Bryan looks at Eddie.

He shakes his head. "Your father stopped by yesterday looking for you. He was worried, after Shawn's death. He may be back tonight. He said things are still coming through the portals and they've been trying to monitor them, but there's not enough of us to track them and keep the woods and townsfolk safe by patrolling. He did say they've seen some freaky stuff going on."

Faith keeps staring at me and my mom with a strange look on her face.

"A succubus?" Faith asks, for what seems like the thousandth time. "Really?"

"You saw what I did. Can anything else make

sense? I'm accepting you're a witch, aren't I?"

She holds up her hand. "I accept it, I'm just not processing it well is all."

"Oh, how could I forget the story in the graveyard." My words slightly run together. Yeah, I've had a bit too much to drink, and the sandwich Bryan fixed wasn't enough to soak up all the beers.

"I'll tell that story." Bryan pats my hand, squeezes it, and pulls it to his lap.

Faith watches the interaction and gives me a WTH kind of stare. A redness seeps into my cheeks, and I'll be expected to explain things to her later about Bryan, but I'm not too sure what I will say. '*Oh, hey, yeah, you know, Faith, I have these attraction type of abilities, and I think they are working on Bryan, but it feels so right with him—oh, and I hope that he will come to Asteria with us so we can live happily ever after.*' I'd rather that conversation remain in my head.

"Yeah, Asteria!" I pipe up after Bryan finishes telling them about the blue men, I mean the men and women with blue auras.

"We'd better cut her off," Faith says.

"No, I'm fine," I insist, and turn to Mom. "You said you had one part of the key, but we need the other part. What the hell was that about?"

Finally, a sober moment had gotten the best of me remembering the cemetery.

Mom had sat quiet the entire time, but leans back, takes a deep breath and exhales. "According to legend, and a witch I once knew, you can only go back to the place from which you came if you have the power source that brought you over in the first place. Being ten at the time, I didn't know what that meant. When I came with my parents, I didn't realize the staff and stone my father carried were the key to bringing us here, and the only key that could also get us home."

"You have the staff?" Bryan asks, pointing to the walking stick.

She nods. "When I returned to town, it found me. It ended up in the Saint's Grove Historical Museum because they dated it as an older artifact of unknown origin, believing it belonged to a Native American medicine man. When I read the explanation on the little card, I laughed so loud, the curator hushed me. I'm sure I looked like an idiot, crying over an old 'Indian' staff, but I knew it was my father's instantly."

"How'd you get it out?" I ask. "Was the stone gone already?"

She shakes her head. "It was intact. The stone sat on top of the staff, as it had all those years ago. I couldn't let the only thing I had left of my father be stuck in some museum. It belonged with me. This was before I even knew of it being a key. I wanted it simply because it had belonged to him, so I did what everyone else does when they want something badly enough. I stole it back."

I laughed. "You stole from the museum? What'd you do? Hide it under your shirt and walk out with no one noticing?" The staff is too huge to do that.

"I broke in at night, Daughter," she says. "It was a fiasco. I'm an awful thief. The alarm sounded as soon as I busted in the backdoor window, and I panicked. I almost left, but then I thought I could make it out before the police got there, or the inhabitants upstairs rose from their sleep."

"Were you caught?" I ask.

"No, but they did sic their dogs on me, after I'd been hiding in the woods. I raced it into the cemetery, running in on some witch ritual. A young girl scared the dogs away, allowing me to run into the mountains with my staff. Soon after, I met your father. He always loved my 'walking stick', as he called it."

"What happened to the stone?"

Bryan squeezes my hand. "Calm down."

I didn't realize I was getting worked up over the story. The night gets late and after the whirlwind of the last few days I'm pooped, but still determined to get to Asteria.

"Sorry," I mumbled.

Mom holds the cloak in her arms and brings it to her face. "Remember the large price I paid for the cloak?"

"You traded the stone for the cloak?" The strain in my eyes start to cause a throbbing headache, and I realize that my mouth remains open entirely too long.

She nods. "I was distraught over your father's death and having to give you up. I needed to hide from prying eyes. I needed to be no one, and that was the price I paid to have it."

I stare at her, disbelief flooding my mind. "But,

by that time, you knew it was the key?"

"The witch that made the cloak for me told me it was the key to my home. It was the young witch I first saw in the cemetery a couple years before that."

"Who was it?" Faith asks.

"Maureen Suzuki is her name. She was powerful and foolish. No one else would help me, as it's against coven rules, so I went to her. She said she would help me in exchange for money, but since I didn't have any, she agreed to take the stone...the Latizite stone. It's rare, since it doesn't come from Earth, and she would be able to get the money she desired for it." She laughs. "She wanted money to go to Cancun with her friends."

I roll my eyes. "Cancun? She sold the rare stone for a trip to Cancun?"

Mom shrugs.

"It's against coven rules to sell spells of any kind," Faith says. "Her name is vaguely familiar. She must have been powerful. I've never seen a cloak like that. It's amazing." Faith touches it. "It's kept its power for so long. I'll never be able to do anything remotely like that in my lifetime."

"Where is she?" I ask. "Where did she sell the stone?"

Mom sighs. "She left town 12 years ago. I don't know where she went, but I'm sure the stone had to be sold somewhere locally. She needed the money to leave town, so I'm assuming she sold it nearby."

Faith's gaze trains on the south wall of the bar. "I think I might know where it could possibly be."

Chapter Sixteen
Day Five

Ana Benton's store, *Some Jems*, is next door to mine, and like me, she inherited it. Faith's excitement the previous evening caught me off guard. She's looking at this as some kind of adventure, and maybe it is, but to me, it's finding my rightful place—the place where I belong most, where I'll find the happiness I've been searching for all my life.

The sun hasn't even bared its first rays. We won't be able to go to Ana's place until 9 AM. Last night, she said we could come in this morning. I must have sounded like a madwoman on the phone. I can only imagine what she may be thinking. *Oh, crazy Ellie wants to see gems when the Apocalypse is happening outside.*

Mom sleeps in Grandpa's old room, Faith's on the couch, Eddie's downstairs, and Bryan's next to me on my bed. Faith's expression, after we discussed and prepared the sleeping arrangements, told me I had a lot of explaining to do. Eddie didn't seem at all surprised. I still feel guilty allowing Eddie to sleep on the kitchen floor. I did give him ample blankets and pillows, but it can't be too comfortable. He refuses to go home, though—overprotective bastard.

I turn to Bryan; he's awake staring at me. He brushes the few strands of hair from my face and smiles.

"Can't sleep either, huh?"

I shake my head. "Too much on my mind."

He pulls me into his arms and I lay on his chest, listening to him breathing in rhythm to his heart. It soothes my wary soul. He smells like my body soap, cucumber melon. I'm not complaining: I love that smell, but I do miss his musty, earthy natural scent. Perhaps I shouldn't have allowed him to shower.

"I understand. There's a lot going on. More than we probably know."

"Yes, there certainly is," I say. "Too bad your dad didn't come by to give us a progress report on the happenings in town."

"Yeah, I know, but my mom called to check on me, after I recharged my phone. Dad kept telling her I was fine, but she hadn't seen my car in the driveway all week and was worried. I forgot I had left it in the alley. It's probably either been destroyed or towed." He chuckles.

"I've never met your mom." I try to remember any town event – concert, play, or farmer's market she may have been to, but I've never seen her around. "Was she at graduation?"

"No, she wasn't. She hasn't left her house in more

than ten years. It's probably a good thing. I think she is out of range of the chaos surrounding us."

I can't imagine being stuck inside all the time. "Never? Not even to the grocery store?"

"Nope. Dad handles all the shopping. She's not left the house since…ever since my brother left." He chokes up.

"Your brother? I didn't know you have a brother." I lean on his chest. He kisses my forehead.

"He's older. He graduated five years before me, and left town. He didn't tell anyone he was going. He packed his things and vanished one summer day, leaving behind the truck my dad had bought him."

I see the pain in his eyes. "Were you close?"

As soon as I ask, I feel guilty. Perhaps he's not ready to talk about it.

"We were close. Rob, his name is Rob, always looked after me. He'd take me everywhere with him—hiking, fishing, canoeing. Even though I was his kid brother, he was never afraid to be seen in public with me. He didn't have many friends. Dad always tried to push him into sports, but Rob refused. He rebelled a lot, and there was constant fighting and turmoil in the house. He always tried to shield me from it, like asking me to draw him a picture—I loved to sketch, and he knew that—but the fighting was loud enough that no amount of shielding could prevent me from hearing it."

"That's awful. The fighting, I mean. I didn't know you sketched, though."

"I stopped a long time ago. It reminded me of

someone I could never be. After Rob left, Mom was never the same. She felt she had lost a part of herself, and she didn't know how else to handle it. She was afraid to leave the house because she'd convinced herself Rob would come home and she wanted to be there for him. She developed agoraphobia, I guess. Dad was angry at first, and would tell her she was crazy, that she needed help. Soon, he accepted it and did everything outside of the house he could. Sometimes, he'd stay at pack members' houses, unable to stand being with Mom anymore."

I'm perplexed by the idea of an agoraphobic werewolf. "How does she change then...into a wolf? Isn't it hard to change in the house?"

"She's not a werewolf," he says. "Dad fell in love with a human, but his genes were more dominant, and my brother and I are like him. Someone told me males tend to take to the wolf gene more than females, which explains why there are more male werewolves." He pauses, and I remain silent, moving up and down with his breathing chest. "My mother told me she prayed for both of us to be girls. Dad was happy to have boys, of course.

"It affected Dad more, though, Rob leaving. He tried harder to shape me into the man he felt I should be. He pushed me into sports—all of them. Later, after the change, he named me his successor, meaning I would be the Alpha of the Pack after he was gone. That made me the Beta for the pack in town. The elders have their own hierarchy, I'm sure."

"You resented it?"

He nods. "I became tired of all the demands. I could never be myself, and when I had the chance to go to college, I jumped on it. It was my opportunity to get out of this place and have a bit of peace, for a while at least."

"Why did you come back?"

"I hoped things would be different. Mom needed me, or she told me as much every day when she called. Plus, this is the life I always knew, and I didn't know where to go or what to do after college. I'm not exactly normal, and our kind is here. I envied my brother his bravery for going rogue. Maybe I'm weak."

I shake my head. "You're not weak."

"I returned, started work at Richards Industries as a graphic designer, as far from the mines as I could get, and decided to keep to myself. My Dad was happy when I returned, but I told him I renounced the position of Beta and would no longer be a part of the pack."

"He didn't take it well, did he?"

"No, not at all. He took Shawn under his wing and left me alone. He hadn't spoken to me until this event happened."

"Nothing from your brother, Rob?"

"The month I graduated, I received a letter postmarked from Seattle…so far away. Rob kept track of me somehow. He apologized for taking off and said leaving me was his only regret.

"Did he ever give any reason for leaving?"

"He wrote he didn't belong in the pack, that he's

gay, and Dad couldn't accept it. Dad asked him to leave and never return, so he did."

"That's awful. I feel so bad for your brother."

"He said he was happy. He found a mate."

"That's better then."

"Rob wrote he'd love to see me again. He asked me to send him one of my sketches. He gave me his address in Seattle, but I haven't heard from him since."

"That was only a few months ago, wasn't it? Didn't you graduate in June or July?"

"Close. I graduated in May, but I stayed in the apartment through July."

"Did you write him back?"

He shakes his head. "No, I haven't."

"Why not?" I hope his feelings aren't what his fathers were. "Are you upset he's gay?"

He looks at the ceiling and shrugs. "I could care less that he's gay. That's not important. I'm glad he's happy. It took a great burden from me when he wrote that. It's that it's been a long time, and I'm afraid he'd be disappointed in me for the choices I've made. I did the exact opposite of him. I followed Dad's orders, even when it made me miserable, whereas Rob stood up for what he believed in. He became the person he wanted to be, when I was only a follower. I suppose I'm ashamed."

"You're not following him anymore. You left the pack, right?"

He nods. "Yes, but I'm still here...in Saint's Grove."

"We all make choices that sometimes aren't what we want. I came back to run this bar at the request of my grandfather, even though he knew I despised it here. Now, I know why he wished it so, but we are both so young and have new choices to make."

"Are you still unhappy in Saint's Grove?"

I smile. "It's a bit more bearable now, despite the craziness."

He stares at me for a moment, a look that sends a wave of warmth through my body. "You saved me, you know. Seeing you every day at the bar, working that cute behind off."

I pat his chest. "Now I know you're lying. My butt is as flat as a pancake."

He squeezes it and I squeak, then cover my mouth. "I beg to differ." He smiles.

"That's not fair." His lips cover mine before I can protest any more of the actions his hands start performing. His gentle kiss becomes deeper and I moan.

He backs away and points to the door. "Shh."

The walls are thin, and every noise we make will carry throughout the small, cramped apartment. The last thing that Mom or Faith want to wake to is us fooling around, I'm sure.

I sigh, as I run my hand through his hair. "I wish we could be alone somewhere. I feel so crowded here, with everyone's eyes on us."

"You and me both. I'd give anything for one more time in the open night air with you by my side again."

Hearts Aligning

He kisses me once more and trails down my neck with his mouth. I relax my body into the soft mattress and imagine being alone with him in the night air. His hands discover my body for the second time, and his touch brings a shiver through me. We adore each other in silence, and it's a feeling I could enjoy every morning with him, if only we can remain together through this wild adventure in which we find ourselves.

He rises slowly up my body, kissing me along the way, and stares into my eyes. "I could be happy here with you. Here in Saint's Grove—with you."

Chapter Seventeen
Day Five

My head swirls with excitement and confusion; excitement because Bryan opened up to me, and confusion because I'm unsure if Bryan would want to go to Asteria, if we actually have that chance anymore. My doubt about that grows by the second.

"Are you going to eat anything?" Faith asks, waving a plate of eggs and toast in the air like a madwoman. She's lucky it didn't all plop onto the floor.

"Thanks." I take the plate out of her erratic hands and sit at the bar. Mom sits next to me, also enjoying her breakfast.

"I was starving," Mom says, with her mouth partially filled. The cloak sits on the stool next to her. She brings it everywhere, even when she goes to the bathroom. I suppose she's so accustomed to wearing it that it's like a second skin. She even throws it over her head if she sees passersby walking next to the bar. She's also been quiet around Eddie and Faith. She engages in the conversations when asked a question, but she's not as chatty as she was in the cabin with me.

I glance at the bird clock on the wall over the bar. Every hour, a different bird tells me what time it is by their unique chirps. It annoys some regulars, but I always shut them up by threatening to replace it with a cat clock that meows instead. "It's almost time."

"It's so exciting, isn't it?" Faith claps her hands together like a crazed teen. She stands across from me, eating while leaning against the bar corner. "I have a feeling we'll find it, Ellie. Don't worry."

I watch her eyes light up. I don't think she understands what will happen if we do find it—I'll leave here. Does she realize?

I watch Bryan bring out a huge plate of eggs and sit next to Eddie. He must have at least 10 of them on there. Must be nice to have a werewolf's metabolism. Now I know why Eddie never gained weight while eating like a friggin' cow all the time.

"Got enough on your plate there, Bry?" Faith asks.

"Not nearly enough, Fai. Why don't you go back into the kitchen and whip us up some more?"

"Why don't you wiggle your cute little wolfy tail and I might?" Faith sticks her tongue out at him.

We all laugh.

"I, um, do you mind if I stay upstairs?" Mom peers at the door to the apartment.

I'm confused. "You know what the stone looks like, though. How are we supposed to find the right one without you?"

"It's a round sphere, cobalt blue with gold strands throughout, sprinkled with black dust. It looks like a lapis, but the difference being the black dust."

"We can find it, Ellie," Faith says. "Your mom can stay here and rest."

"You're the one who should be resting, Faith." I point to her bandaged side.

"It's better. We're only going next door, you know."

"I guess if we find similar stones, Ana can let us bring them over for you to look at. Are you sure you don't want to go?"

She shakes her head. "I'm overwhelmed. I haven't spoken with this many people in a long time. I guess it's weighing on me."

I smile and pat her hand. "Okay. We won't be long."

I wonder if something else bothers Mom. It's true. She's not used to all of these people. I hadn't imagined her anxiousness being around us. She's way out of her element. No fairies or nymphs playing in her garden or stealing her vegetables.

Bryan clears his throat. "I think you girls can handle this."

I furrow my brow. "What? You, too?"

This morning it was too crowded and now it feels like it's too few.

He grins. "I was hoping to check on Mom and my house; make sure everything is all right, and hurry back here." He kisses my forehead. "Eddie will stay.

I promise I'll be back in an hour, tops."

I hop off the barstool. "Okay, it looks like it's you and me, Faith."

Bryan picks me up in a huge bear hug and twirls me around, kissing me on the mouth before setting me down.

"See you soon," he whispers in my ear and heads to the front door. Eddie follows, locking the door after he leaves.

"That was dramatic," Faith says. "And more than a little bizarre."

"I'm going upstairs." Mom grabs her cloak and heads to the apartment door.

"We'll be back soon." I wave, but she's already in the hallway.

"I'll do the dishes." Eddie gathers the plates.

Faith looks at me, her eyes widening. "Are you ready?"

I nod. "Ready as I'll ever be, I guess."

We walk through the kitchen. Eddie stops what he's doing and follows as we head out the back door to the bar. The morning light hits the woods at the right angle and makes them appear to sparkle. I breathe in and smell the rustic scent.

Eddie watches us walk the few steps to Ana's door. "Knock loud when you girls come back. I may be running the water."

"We'll be fine."

"Okay." He closes the door.

I raise my hand to knock but Faith stops me.

"What?"

"What?" she repeats. "We haven't had a moment alone, yet. Bryan's been all gushy over you and hogging you away these last few days. What's going on?"

I shrug. "What do you mean? You see it."

Trying to come to terms with my feelings makes it hard for me to share too much of them, I guess.

Faith rolls her eyes and crosses her arms. "Give me a break. One minute I'm being bitten by a wolf, and the next you two are shacking up for a romantic getaway in the mountains. Bryan's been here for two months and not once asked you out. He walks in, has a beer, and leaves, and now you two are an item?"

"You have a lot to say about it."

"Do you think it has something to do with your new found powers? Does that scare you?"

Tears well behind my eyelids. "Oh, God, you have no idea. What if that's it? What if he never liked me like that before now? I mean, he says otherwise. Bryan says I saved him, that he came to the bar every day to see me working. He said I inspired him to carry on."

"Yeah, I knew you needed to get that out." Faith purses her lips. "You've been holding that in, haven't you?"

She hugs me. I fall into her embrace and relief washes over me. "I have that worry in the back of my head."

"He is cute, you know. For a werewolf." She scrunches up her nose and we laugh.

"Yeah, I know."

"Do you feel better now?"

I nod. "A little, but I still don't know what I'm going to do."

Faith raises her eyebrows. "So, did you guys...you know?"

"You had to go there?"

"It's me…Faith. Of course, I have to go there. Duh!"

I cross my arms. "That's none of your business."

"I'll take that as a yes."

"Take it any way you want. But, what if we do find this stone and I have a way back to where I belong? I finally found a great guy, and this thing happens."

"What do you mean? You'll leave here for good?" Faith's mouth hangs open.

I shrug. "Maybe it's where I belong." Faith closes her mouth and several seconds tick by; a knotty feeling bubbles in my stomach.

The corner of her tightened lips curve upward. "Your mom says countless amazing things about it…the world she's from. Have you talked to her about your doubts or what you want?"

Relief washes through me. The silence felt unbearable...Faith's not angry with me for wanting to leave. "I'm getting acquainted with her. It's like learning everything for the first time. I feel like a little kid asking her question after question, and I see her getting wary." I look up at the back apartment window. Mom stands there looking at her mountain. "I know she wants to go home, and I honestly think she would thrive there. It's a different atmosphere, and she'd likely live longer."

"And you want to be with her longer? How would you feel leaving us? Leaving Eddie and me behind? Or Bryan?"

I sigh, completely frustrated. "Ugh. Why does everything seem so difficult now? It's crazy to hope we could go together? All of us? I'm not sure that's what Bryan would want. He has family here, and so do you. Even Eddie seems happy in Saint's Grove."

"I can't answer for them, but I'm not sure about going to a different world, Ellie. It would be fun and adventurous, and your mom makes it sound like paradise, truly, but we are creatures of habit. Here, I know what I'm getting. I'm comfortable here where I know there are my kind. I've even thought about joining my mother's coven and learning more of our craft." Faith shrugs. "With everything that's been happening, maybe being an informed, trained witch might be a good idea."

Wetness threatens to drip down my cheeks at the thought of life without Faith. "I feel like I'm losing my best friend. I do think being a witch is cool, though, for the record."

Faith hugs me and tears trickle down her cheek. "I'll always love you, no matter what you decide, Ellie. We have to give you that option though."

We embrace for a few moments, then step apart and give each other a sad smile. She squeezes my hand. "Are you ready?"

I nod, and she reaches behind me, giving the door

a firm knock.

We both turn to the door and listen to the sound of footsteps nearing us.

Ana greets us with a smile. "Hey, Ellie, Faith. Come on in."

The first thing I notice about Ana is her aura. It's not exactly yellow, but more of a fiery orange-red color. She's adventurous and daring, or so her aura tells me. I'm getting better at this, I think, although I don't know quite what that makes Ana, but she's more than human.

A cluttered work area greets us as we walk through the back door. Stacks of boxes line the walls in the back room, and a small, wooden work desk rests in the far corner. An old boom box with both a CD and cassette tape player sits on the desk. Does anyone still have tapes to play in those things? Even CDs are becoming obsolete these days.

As we move through the back and into the front of the store, we see the broken windows and the security bars and door. I can't even begin to know what happened here, but I'm glad that Ana weathered it.

Ana turns to us. "What can I do for you girls? It's been a crazy week, huh?"

"The craziest. I'm glad to see you're well, Ana."

"I'm glad you both are, too."

"We are looking for a stone," Faith interjects. "It's a sphere, the size of my hand, blue—"

"Cobalt blue," I interrupt.

"With gold lines throughout it and black speckles

throughout."

Ana nods as if she knows exactly what we're talking about. "Like a Lapis Lazuli. One of the prettiest stones I've ever seen. Did you know that the ancient Egyptians used it as eyeshadow? Can you believe that? Such a pretty stone to be ground into a powder for an adornment, right?"

"Yes, kind of like that. It would have been sold roughly twenty-three years ago?"

"It was sold to my grandmother a long time ago. She kept it hidden because she liked it so much. She said it always calmed her." Ana clasps her hands together and cracks her knuckles.

Faith cups her mouth. "Oh My God. You have it?"

Ana shakes her head as a cease forms in her brow. "Not anymore. I sold it last week, a few days before The Event, to a man from out of town. A collector of sorts; said he was in search of rare lapis. I'm so sorry."

Chapter Eighteen
Day Five

"I'm sorry, Ellie," Faith says for what seems like the twentieth time. "Seriously, I know this meant a lot to you and your mom."

Ana closes the door behind us. We walk slowly back to the bar. I have to admit, I'm disappointed and desperate, but not defeated. I know the bookstore has some pretty strange reads, and I'm thinking maybe, just maybe, Irene, the owner, can help me. "I want to go and check out *Sherlock's Tomes*."

Faith rolls her eyes at me, something she seems to be doing more these days. "Ya think Irene will have some reference books on eccentric stone collectors?" She sighs. "Ellie, I got to tell you, even if she does, I don't think we'll find anything on this mysterious guy. He's probably left town by now."

"I've got to try *something*. Mom wants to go home. You should see her light up when she talks about Asteria, and there may not be another chance for this to happen."

Faith shrugs and looks at the sidewalk, as if in deep thought. After a moment, she says, "I guess I could make some calls, see if anyone knows anything. Maybe Mom heard something through the 'witch-vine'. She always seems up on the local gossip."

I'm beginning to feel better, but I'm still worried. "Okay, you do that and I'll head over to see if Irene is there."

"Do you think that's a good idea? Maybe you should wait until Bryan comes back so he can go with you."

I hate the idea of waiting for a man to protect me, but these aren't normal times. "Fine. I'll wait for him, but he'd better be back soon. We're running out of time, Faith."

"I know." She pats my arm, and bangs on the door.

Eddie opens it and lets us in. "Well? Did you find it?"

I shake my head.

"Sorry. It's too bad it wasn't there. I was hoping you'd find it at Ana's place."

"Oh, it was there until last week when some guy bought it," Faith tells him. "It's a sore subject."

"Has Bryan called?" I ask.

Eddie shakes his head.

"Why don't you go up and talk with your mom?" Faith suggests. "We can hang down here for a while. When Bryan returns, I'll send him up."

"Okay, thanks." I squeeze her hand and head to my apartment.

Mom sits at my circular kitchen table with the

box of photos we found from the basement. She flips through the photo albums pages. "You were such a beautiful child." She turns the page. "So full of life. I'd watch from afar, you know. Sometimes, I'd wait in the woods outside the school and watch you during recess."

I'm really not sure what to say, so I simply thank her.

I sit across from her and pick up the closest album. I remember the day the pictures were taken - Grandpa had brought me to the park and kept snapping pictures of me. I must have been eight or nine.

"Some of these I had completely forgotten about. Grandpa didn't take many pictures, but when he did, he snapped a lot at once."

I glance up at my mother and try to put myself in her shoes. "It must have been hard trying to keep track of my life from far away. I can't imagine what you have been through."

"It was difficult to stay away, and your grandfather made it harder on me sometimes. He didn't understand why I was so distant and I couldn't tell him the truth. The only one who ever knew was your father."

She sighs and stares at the photo album. "People are scared of the unknown, which leads them to fear us or think we are crazy."

"I understand."

"You didn't find the stone, did you?"

"No, we didn't. Ana said she sold it about a week

ago. At least she thinks it was the same stone. She said a collector came from out of town for it, but she didn't get his name. He paid cash, and a lot, apparently."

Mom rubs her cloak that lays thrown over her chair.

"It was pretty. I can see how it would be valuable to a collector. He probably had never seen anything like it here. I should never have given it up."

I feel as though I've failed her, and my throat clenches. "I'm sorry. I'm going to look around town and see what I can find out. Maybe he's still here, or there's a record of him somewhere. They have reference books at *Sherlock's Tomes* I can search. Maybe he is a huge, famous collector."

Mom grabs my hand. "It's all right, Ellie. We tried our best. Let's get through the next couple of days and move on. It's the best we can do."

"Move on to what? Are you going back up to your mountain home, away from us again?"

Her brow furrows at my questions, as if she doesn't understand. "That is my home, isn't it? You can come up any time and see me, of course. Things are different now. We can build a relationship, but please have patience with me. I've been alone for a long time."

"What would've happened had we found the stone? What would Asteria have been like for us?"

Her eyes light up once again. "Oh, you would be so happy there, Ellie. We would have taken our rightful place in the family castle and ruled side-by-side over the land and the people."

"What does that entail, actually? What are we ruling over if it's such a peaceful place? You were so young when you were there last, so how do you know things aren't different now?"

She put the photo album down. "Father always seemed happy. He would settle marriage proposals or children's requests. He'd be the one to allow it or put it off for a better time, whatever the situation called for. Even in a peaceful place, such as Asteria, direction is still needed at times. He also planned celebrations, and assigned tasks and help in the fields or workhouses. We all pitched in to get things done that would benefit us all."

She walks toward the window. "I remember one time Father made us all get up early one morning and help in the fields. We had a torrential rain the evening before, and as a town, we all worked together to gather all the good crops we could save. That evening, we had a grand feast. Even in the throes of misfortune, we made it one of thanks and blessing. So it was things like that he needed to decide. Although we were called royalty, it was more of a leadership role."

The image of a small community edges its way into my mind...one that reminds me of an older village that existed a hundred years ago where people bartered things with their neighbors, and everyone helped each other when a barn needed to be built or fields plowed. Those times seem simpler, but things have certainly changed.

"Sounds like a great place to live, and a wonderful plan to live by—sharing and helping. It's a wonder we've survived so long as a species here with war and poverty. Well, the humans, I mean. It's so hard to believe I'm from two different worlds. One here, on Earth, my father's land, and one in a faraway world that sounds like a fairytale dream."

"I guess we shouldn't dredge up what can never be. I wish I hadn't raised your hopes now that I'm unable to show you where we're from. You could be right; maybe it's different now. Maybe after we left, things changed. I hope that's not the case, though. I like to remember it the way it was."

Although she stops talking, it seems she wants to say more. She doesn't.

I shake my head. "No, it was good to learn of it and listen to your description. I'm glad I know about Asteria, and I hope it's the same way, too."

She smiles and looks at the forest once more.

I want to help Mom get back to Asteria. Sitting here listening to stories isn't going to do it, but action will. "I'm going to the bookstore. Maybe I'll uncover something that will click. I don't want to wait much longer to head there. It'll be dark before we know it."

She nods. "Please be careful. It may be best to ride this thing out in here, away from danger. The portals are still open; things may be lingering nearby."

I look around my apartment. "It does feel safe in here, doesn't it? I guess I'm thankful a portal didn't open up inside my place. That would have been disastrous."

"Normal things usually do feel safe. I feel safe in the cabin, but I know that anything could get in there if it wanted to, but it's where I feel most comfortable."

"I'm glad you are here with us, though."

She turns and gives me a sad smile. "Me, too."

I leave the apartment, walking downstairs to the bar. Faith and Eddie play cards at one of the tables.

"Want to join us?" Faith asks. "I didn't find anything of substance when I called Mom. No one recalls the stranger in town last week. He must have come for the stone."

"No, I'm going outside to check some things out."

As I head out, Faith frowns and places her cards face down on the table. "You said you'd wait for Bryan."

"Yeah, Ells, wait and he'll be here," Eddie says. "Or, if you want, I'll go with you?"

"Nah, it looks fine out there, almost normal," I say, peering out the window. "It's quiet. Besides, I don't want to wait any longer. I'm feeling antsy stuck in here. Maybe I'll take a short walk and check some stores out."

"Okay, but don't go far and stay where we can see you." Eddie follows me to the door. "I'll lock it when you leave and keep watch."

"Eddie, you don't have to. I'll be fine."

He looks around the center of town and nods. He helps me open the door and closes it behind me. It looks eerier than it had from behind my bar door. *Some Jems'* busted windows look worse from the front. A few other stores suffered damage, as well. I wonder what's happened to all the storeowners and workers. Did most leave town? We probably should leave as well, get out for a few days, but I guess we have been lucky not to run into any more demons or evil entities.

Sherlock's Tomes sits on the corner of the town square. I see the bookstore and head across the open grassy path, watching every direction. A few cars line the street next to the bookstore, around the corner. One car drives by slowly, and I look to see if it's Bryan, but it's not.

Before I cross the street to get to the bookstore, I notice a familiar-looking man standing by a car on the corner. He wears a light, black coat and a baseball cap. He notices me and I immediately feel uncomfortable. I'd forgotten about my appealing powers and I concentrate, breathing in deeply, on being normal and invisible.

That doesn't work. He still stares, and as I get closer to the sidewalk, I see why he's staring. I can't stop gawking at him, and my mouth drops open. Like mine, his green aura beckons me to him. Our eyes meet for longer than a moment, and I stand still frozen on the sidewalk; it feels like time ceases to exist.

Hearts Aligning

It's the same guy from the bar on the night of the event...the odd one that didn't buy anything and hit on me in the weirdest of ways...which makes our chance encounter all the more bizarre, but oddly electrifying. He breaks our gaze and rushes around the car, fumbling with his keys to get behind the wheel.

"Wait," I wave at him like a fool. He can't hear me since a truck drives past as he gets into his car. As he starts his engine, he's looking over his shoulder to see if any cars are coming. He pulls away from the curb, and I do the only thing I can think of—I run in front of his car. He doesn't see me. His brakes squeal and I feel the impact of the bumper against my thigh. I fall back, hitting the back of my head on the asphalt, and a fuzzy feeling swarms in my head.

I open my eyes to find him standing above me. When he speaks, I focus on his mouth. "Why did you do a foolish thing like that?" he asks.

An incoherent sensation forms in my head, and my ears are ringing. He becomes a large, blurring mass and fades into complete darkness.

Chapter Nineteen
Day Six

Coldness seeps through my skin and goosebumps form all over. My head aches and my heartbeat's loud rhythm pounds in my ears.

"What?" The scratchy voice escaping my lips sounds like that of an old woman. I open my eyes to see a dark brown cushion. As I try to turn over, I realize my hands burn and tingle as if they are overcoming a numbing sensation. They're behind my back and tied together, as are my legs. I roll off the couch and land face first on a carpet with a thud. "Ow!"

"Easy there," a male's voice says.

I turn over on my side, which sends a sharp pain down the length of my body. A narrow beam of light from a hallway shines into the room, and the windows seem too dark for it to be light outside. "What happened?"

"You hit my car." A tall figure comes into view and blocks the light from the hallway. "Or rather, my car hit you. You've been out all night."

All night? It must be early morning, but the sunlight doesn't penetrate the room. How could I have stayed here all night...wherever here is. I've lost more time. Time...I know it's important, but I can't comprehend why...things are so unclear.

"What..." My train of thought disappears. The man's voice perplexes me. The last thing I remember was walking toward the bookstore and...

Two big arms pull me off the floor and sit me on the couch. "That hurts, dammit."

A bandage drops a little over my eye, reminding me that my head pounds like it's been hit with a sledgehammer. This man tried to dress my head, but did a poor job, as the binding isn't tight enough.

Time. We needed to find something, and I was out looking for it...it's all right there, but I can't retrieve it.

"I said you bloody well ran right out in front of my car," the strange shadow man says. I can't make out his features in the dim light.

"Who—?" I ask.

"You! You ran in front of my car like a crazed woman." He sits on the coffee table in front of me. His face is close to mine. "Now, my little, crazy succubus, who's apparently never seen a car before, how the bloody hell did you get here? And how did you disguise yourself on our first encounter?"

"Who are you?" I finish the question I was trying to ask. The events slowly ease into my head. The word succubus triggers memories. I'm a succubus and we were searching for a stone. Mother, Faith, Eddie, and Bryan. Surely, they must be looking for me.

This man stood by the car—his aura was green. It's the man that was in front of the bookstore. "You're like me." I look closer at him and see his jade tint in the dim light.

He grins. "Very good. How rude of me not to introduce myself, again. My apologies. I'm Desmon, or Desmond, as I'm referred to in England, which is by far better than this place. Much more civilized than your America." He rubs his head, and his cap moves with the motion. "We met once and you hid your true nature from me somehow. I suspect witchcraft. Now, how did you get through the portal? Are there more of you that came over? You were here prior to the opening of the portals, so I need to know how."

I shake my head, confused by what he's asking. His words make no sense to me, and his accent doesn't sound entirely British, but he enjoys using some common British slang words.

He sits back, crosses his arms, and exhales loudly, obviously annoyed with my lack of answers.

"You seem disoriented. I suppose you hit your head harder than I thought. I don't have time for this. Do you even know who you are?"

"I, um…" words fumble from my mouth. "Yes, dammit, I know who I am!"

"You're not from Asteria, are you? It's been a while, but I'm positive my kind wouldn't talk so abruptly." He turns on a lamp next to the couch. The place behind my eyes aches. "Who are you?"

I blink and squint, the light stabbing my retinas. I wish he would untie my hands so I can cover my eyes.

Desmon sighs. "It would be polite to tell me your name, since I've already introduced myself."

"Ellie. I'm Ellie, and can you please untie me? My hands ache."

"Where are you from, Ellie?"

"Here. Right here…in Saint's Grove." I widen my eyes and wiggle my arms at him. "Why the hell did you tie me up?"

"You're from here?" He raises his eyebrows.

"That's what I said!"

"Who are your parents? Who else survived the massacre long ago?"

His questions are relentless. I don't know if I should answer him. Why the hell did he tie me up, and his aura…it's a darker shade of green for someone from such a peaceful place.

He stands and taps his finger against his chin. "Ellie, you and I are similar people. I could tell that right away. You're drawn to me, as I am to you. Do you know why that is?"

I shake my head. "If we are so 'drawn' to each other, then why did you jump into the car to take off?"

"A fair question." He paces the carpet in front of me. I notice the family pictures on the wall behind him, next to the big screen TV. He's not in any of those pictures. I look around and know he doesn't belong here at all. The air-conditioning kicks on and a putrid, decaying smell pumps through the vents. Oh, this isn't a good sign.

He's tall, with dark hair tucked under his generic blue denim baseball cap. He has to be around my age…maybe, I'm not a good judge of that. He's probably older than Mother. His chestnut eyes sparkle each time he moves his head to the side and the light from the lamp catches them. His perfect chin and clear skin make him look glamourous. What's the male version of a succubus? An incubus. I hadn't even thought about that; he's the male version of me and Mom, with the alluring traits to boot.

He's still pacing the room. "I wasn't expecting another of our kind, and I don't know you. You could've been sent to kill me, for all I know."

I narrow my eyes. "Why would any of our kind be sent here for you?"

"Because I'm the one who brought the royal family over, of course."

His words hit me like an anvil to the sternum. He brought my mother over, along with her family, to their slaughter?

"It wasn't my intention that things occurred as they did, but it happened nevertheless."

"What do you mean?"

"You didn't let me finish telling you why we are drawn to each other. Impatient, aren't you?"

I'm briefly confused by the quick turn of the conversation. "Why are we drawn to each other?"

I can't say at this moment I'm drawn to him, but I remember the feeling in front of the bookstore. There was a connection of some kind, not romantic, but more of a kindred spirit calling.

He switches on another lamp on the other side of the room. "You see my color?"

"Yes." It's the same tinted, dark jungle green I saw as he stood in front of his car.

"It's the same color yours is. We've both fed recently. Am I right?"

Fed…I see Shawn's face in my mind. I didn't think of it as a feeding, but more of an energizing experience, but Desmon is right. I've taken a life, and he knows it. Disgust forms in the pit of my stomach and I want to throw up. I nod.

"See?" He smiles, gesturing between us. "We are the same. We see these humans for what they are—food for our survival. Nothing more than for our pleasure, and to replenish our youth. They are what keeps us alive and young."

I say nothing. His aura screams greed to me. It's a greedy shade of green and I'm ashamed to share that same color with him. Like Mom, I'll never feed again. I try not to crinkle my nose with the pure revulsion of the thought.

"Do you know how long I've been roaming this barbaric world?" When I don't answer, he continues, "Go on, take a guess. How old do I look?"

He sure likes to talk. I see a devilish side to him. He enjoys an audience, apparently, but I don't think his human spectators stay around long enough. Can we take each other's lives, too? The thought hadn't crossed my mind before now, but I wonder if he may be able to kill me.

"You've been here a while, I'm sure, but you look my age."

"Ah, so you're a young one, then. Haven't been feeding that long to look the way you do?" He doesn't wait for my answer before he continues. "Yes, I've been roaming on this plane for more than three centuries, but the people are still as naive today as they were then."

"How did you escape the bloodbath?" I ask, curious about how he survived the attacks that plagued the town all those years ago. "When you came over, I mean."

He points to his head. "I'm smart enough to know when to run. No one was safe back then. It was an atrocity. I was lucky to have made it out of there, and I was faster than the others, so I survived. Well, that's not entirely true. I charmed my way into the arms of a beautiful wolf-woman who helped me out of the massacre. Then I fed on her because I couldn't resist, as she couldn't resist me. I've been living off my charm all this time. It was a blessing here in this world. I was like a god sitting on a throne."

His ego definitely left a sour taste in my mouth. "Why not stay then, since it's so wonderful for you here?"

He shrugs. "I can live forever here, a rich man, full of life, but even that gets boring after a while. Can you imagine living in a place watching everyone dic while you adapt with the changing times and people? It's why I never got close to anyone. They are food, after all. I started doing research on the alignment of the planets and could you believe the event that brought me to this exact place was due to happen again? I can go home now, during this rare window of opportunity."

The things Mother told me surface. I remember her saying her family came through the portal. "You were the one who led them here? The others of your kind? Did you know what would happen?"

"No one knew what would happen, but it was a chance to change things, and we needed to take that chance. I underestimated the situation. Had things gone as planned, I would have immediately returned to Asteria, trapping the royals in this plane, and taken control of the kingdom. But things turned out so much better than expected. In this place there are no rulers; no one to tell us what we must do and how to do it. We make our own decisions."

"I thought it was peaceful there? No fighting, working together...peaceful."

"You didn't know the place, did you? Someone told you stories, but not the entire truth."

I think about Mom being only 10 years old at the time, and maybe Asteria was perfect to her because she was so young and didn't know the way of things. I recall the story of how her father made them all help with the crops and how they rejoiced in it afterwards. Perhaps to her, things were perfect in her 10-year-old eyes; things are always good when you're young, before you know the way of the world.

As he keeps me talking, he's gathering information. I see that now. He's baiting me, and I'm falling for all of it. Maybe I'm as naive as all of his victims were. He's learned to live among us well— he's had centuries of practice.

"Who are your parents?"

Time for me to turn the tables. He's not going to get anything more out of me. "They're dead. My father died the day I was born and my mother died years later."

"And their names?"

I shrug. "I don't know. My mother used a fake name, of course. I never asked her."

He slaps my face. "Don't lie to me. I always know when you're lying. Your aura waves like a flag in the wind."

The sting causes a quick build-up of tears to flow down my cheek.

"You're not protecting anyone by lying. Someone survived that massacre besides me, and you need to tell me who's here."

Chapter Twenty
Day Six

"That wasn't nice." I glare at him. Seriously, that's all I can come up with? I should be cursing and yelling, but he caught me off guard.

He shrugs and resumes pacing. "Being nice doesn't seem to work with you, and I am becoming impatient. Who are your parents? Don't lie this time or the next hit will hurt."

He sits in front of me and watches my eyes. "I was raised by my grandfather," I say through my grinding teeth. "You ass!"

"Truth." He tilts his head. "Who is your grandfather?"

"Gus Whitaker." I hope telling him some truths and skirt around others will appease him. "He raised me from a baby, and he owned the Mountaintop Bar & Grill in town, until his death five years ago. He was human."

I keep my gaze on his chestnut eyes and don't bat a lash.

"He was, but you're not. You know your parents' names though, since he was your grandfather. No?"

"My father was his son, had the same name, but was a Jr. He was human, also."

"One human parent? Interesting. I didn't think that was even possible." He gets up. "I never let a woman live long enough to bear the fruit of our love."

I cringe. What a lovely date he must be.

"Who was your mother?"

I shrug. "I was raised thinking she had died when I was little."

He bends and grabs my collar, pulling me to him. "Who was your mother?" He grips my neck with his other hand and squeezes it. My throat restricts and I gasp. "Tell me now!"

"Lily," I say. "Her name was Lily."

"Lily?" He throws me back onto the couch. My head throbs more after hitting the cushion. A liquid oozes down my forehead. That's not a good sign. He walks toward the window where a little light has begun to creep under the curtain, then turns to face me. "Are you sure? She was merely a little girl. How did she survive?"

I roll my eyes at him.

"No one else survived?"

"No, no one else that she knows of. She didn't think you were here either, so maybe there are more than you think."

"A little girl surviving that massacre…impossible."

I'm done talking. "Look, I've told you everything you want to know, so you can let me go now!"

Desmon laughs. He walks down the hallway, then before disappearing around the corner, turns back to me. "Why would I do a foolish thing like that? Where is she now?"

I stare at him in disbelief. "Do you actually think I'd tell you that?"

He turns and leaves. I struggle with the rope around my wrists as fear gnaws at my gut. The knots are tight. Maybe if I bend I can free my feet. I lean over on the couch and try to reach the ropes wrapped around my feet, determined to find a way out of here.

Moments later, a door creaks open and I know he's coming back. He stands at the entryway, hands behind his back, staring at me.

"You do remind me of her, you know. You have the same hair. She was an awful child, always so needy and clingy. Were you that way as a child?"

I don't answer. He approaches, revealing what was lurking behind his back—another rope and tape. I back into the sofa as far as my body takes me. "Oh, come on." He pushes me face down into the couch and ties my hands to my feet with another rope on top of the ones that already bind me. I'm hogtied now. Fucking great.

"Is this necessary? Two ropes weren't enough?" I ask sarcastically.

He turns me onto my side and unrolls a piece of tape.

"Why? You don't need to do that. Aren't you

going to keep asking questions?" Anything is better than duct tape on my mouth.

"Nope, but I can't have you scream bloody murder while I'm gone, now can I?" He rips a piece free and puts it tightly over my mouth.

"J-J-J-," I say, but I wanted to say *Jerk!*

"There, that's better." He smiles. "You stay put and I'll see you later." He bends and pats my head as if I'm a puppy.

He walks to the front of the house. I listen as he shuts one door and then the front door behind him. It only took him 30 seconds to reach it, so it's not far away from the living room I'm in now. There has to be a way for me to get out of this. I struggle with the ties behind me. They are tight and scrape ruthlessly against my bare skin.

Along with the pain, another emotion slinks into me...fear. It's a surmountable feeling of helplessness and anger mixed together. How will I escape this mess?

Of all the monsters that could get me, it had to be the type that I am.

Hours seem to pass slowly. I manage to roll myself into a corner and pull the curtains on top of me. I keep rolling into the wall, trying to make noise, but it's useless. All I can do is roll around and cause myself more pain and more destruction to this stranger's house. My arms and legs become numb and when I move it feels like a thousand needle pricks are traveling down my body.

My eyes swell with tears, as I think of everyone I care about so much. They are probably going out of their minds right now, and it's all my fault. Why did I have to be so stupid? Had I only waited and not insisted on leaving alone to search for the stone; had I not run out in front of the damned car trying to seek answers from this lunatic, I'd be safe in the bar with Faith, Eddie, Mom, and Bryan.

Desmon isn't going to leave loose ends. I know too much about him and he could care less about me…drawn to him, my ass. Why would outliving other people bother him so much? He's so in love with himself, I can't imagine he'd want anyone to take the attention from him. I take a little comfort in knowing he's trapped here and can't taint others with his stupidity. Maybe he'll be eaten by a vampire or cursed by a witch.

I'd love to see Faith freeze his ass solid. I'd kick the heck out of that giant lump of ice.

The front door squeaks open. I try to dry the tears from my face so I don't give him the satisfaction of knowing I'm upset.

He takes his time, not coming into the living room right away. I hear the clinking of plates and glasses. He's feeding himself in the kitchen…the jerk.

I try to roll as close to the couch as I can, which is a foolish endeavor. I can't even get back up onto the couch, and he'll see the curtains pulled down.

Anger boils up to the surface. I push an end table over—a lamp falls and shatters on the tile floor. That gets his attention: his footsteps grow louder the closer he comes to the living room.

"What are you carrying on about in here?" Desmon walks around the room with a plate in his hand. "Tearing the curtains down and destroying other people's property?" He tosses the plate across the coffee table and reaches down, yanking me up so hard I feel like my limbs will be torn off their sockets. He throws me face down on the couch. He clicks his tongue against the roof of his mouth. "I was planning on being nice to you and allowing you to eat, but you had to go and be awful like this. I can see you're as unruly as your mother was as a child. Maybe you should suffer more."

I whine under the tape, trying my best to argue with him, but I hear him walk out of the room again. Asshole!

He bangs loudly around in the other room...most likely the kitchen. He turns on a TV in that room, raises the volume, laughs here and there, and generally annoys me for a good 30 minutes before returning.

I turn to see him staring at me with his arms crossed.

"I've calmed down and realized we need to get past our differences." He moves around the coffee table, turns me around and loosens the ropes that tie my hands to my legs. The relief is agony as my legs stretch out. "If you want to eat, I'll untie your hands for a while, but you need to promise you won't be stupid." He sits me upright facing the coffee table.

He peels back the duct tape from my mouth. I wince, having expected him to yank it off, but he moves slowly. The tape still feels like it's taking my skin with it.

"Ouch!" I take a deep breath. I stare into his eyes. "Let me go, please." The tears come, and I can't stop them. "I want to go home." I'm losing it. Anger has passed and now I'm begging.

He shakes his head and touches my cheek. I close my eyes, backing away, half expecting him to slap me again. "I can't do that, sweet Ellie, but I have brought you a gift. I think you'll like it."

Desmon smiles. He grabs a paper bag that was on the carpet. I hadn't seen him bring it in, but odors surface from the bag. I smell fried food.

He pulls out a white container. "Do you recognize the box?"

I shake my head.

"Don't you recognize food from your own bar?" He opens the container revealing fries and a cheese sandwich—Eddie's cooking.

"You went to my bar and they let you in?"

He nods. "It wasn't that hard getting in. I don't look threatening, do I? Your cook, Eddie, answered the door, invited me in after I asked for a meal to go, and cooked it for me."

Disgust builds in my stomach. I'm no longer hungry.

"He was worried about you, though. He showed

me a picture and asked if I'd seen you. Did you know he was a wolf before you hired him?"

I shake my head. "Did…was anyone else there?"

He shakes his head. "I gather from our conversation, Eddie and I that is, that some of your other friends were out looking for you, involving the local police, I'm sure. It was quite disappointing not to find Lily there though as I'd hoped. I can imagine the look on her face."

"You can't touch her." I purse my lips. "Please leave them alone. Take me, do whatever you want, but leave them alone."

"You know the irony in this situation? She has something I want, and you fell into my lap, giving me something she wants."

"What are you talking about?"

"When I went to the jewelry store in search of the Latizite, the jeweler told me it had been sold to her grandmother, years ago," Desmon says. "Only the stone, not the staff it was attached to." My stomach drops. "Your mother kept the staff for sentimental reasons, didn't she?"

I frown.

He smiles. "So, I have something she wants and she has something I want."

"You won't find her," I say, hoping she went back up the mountain.

"Oh, I won't have to find her. She'll find me. I left her a message."

I glare at him.

"You know what tastes better than these fried

potatoes?" He puts a french fry into his mouth. "The cook who prepared them."

Chapter Twenty-One
Day Six

A headache pounds me awake and my mind is clouded by haziness. My stomach growls loudly; small achy sounds escape my mouth. I try to muzzle them with my hand, but it's stuck over my head. Both of my hands are trapped above me. I try to yank them down.

"Wakey, wakey," a male voice enters my head. I blink away the haze to see Desmon smiling down at me.

He positions his face inches from mine. "How are you doing this late evening?" He purses his lips out making a convincing duck face. "I'm so terribly sorry about having to drug you, but you wouldn't stop your blabbering. It was dreadfully annoying."

"Drugggged?" My voice crackles, and my lips feel like sandpaper. I try to lick them. "You drugged me?"

He nods, smiling, looking so pleased with himself. "It helped me get some rest after an exhausting afternoon. I was able to move you without complaint. Much nicer quarters, don't you think?"

"Eddie…" The tears come again, remembering how Desmon told me he had killed Eddie.

Desmon backs up. "Oh, not this again. I'll drug you once more if you can't control those awful emotions of yours. I guess that's a downfall to being part human. You're a sniveling mess."

I try to kick him, but my feet are similarly tied to the bottom of the bed.

"Anger." Desmon shakes his head and sighs. "Another worthless human emotion. I'll admit though, it's one I understand better. But if you keep acting like a fool, you'll end up harming your bed mate." He looks past me. I turn to see the object of his gaze. A young woman with a yellow aura lies in the bed next to me, staring at Desmon with an affectionate smile. She's not bound, so she could get up and leave if she wanted.

Oh, hell. No! "What the hell are you doing? Get up and get out of here!"

Desmon laughs. "Isn't she magnificent? I found her wandering the streets tonight and thought what a nice gift she would make for you. You do looked rather parched, you know."

"Desmon, let her go, please."

Desmon walks to the dresser, where he wrings out a washcloth in a bowl of water and brings it to me. "But, it's my gift to you. Don't you know you're supposed to accept gifts graciously? A thank you would be nice."

He pats down my cracked lips with the washcloth

and it feels like he's putting out a fire. I grab the washcloth with my lips for a few seconds before he takes it away.

He grins. "Isn't that better?"

"I…um…" I don't know what to say. I look back at the young girl, whose stare follows Desmon's every move. How does he wield such power over her? Her yellow aura beckons like a siren calling sailors at sea…I'm drawn to her, but not enough to take her life. I don't need her energy to fulfill me, not like Desmon seems to need it.

He caresses my cheek while my head faces away from him, then whispers in my ear. "Go ahead, take her."

"Desmon, can I have some water, please?" I turn to him, imploring him with my gaze.

He leans down to my ear. I feel the tips of his lips on my earlobe. "Once you take her, you'll feel so much better."

"No!" I yell. "I will not take this girl's life! Please let her go!"

He throws the washcloth across the room with such force that it knocks over the bowl of water on the dresser. The girl next to me doesn't flinch.

I don't recognize her from town, but her light yellow aura tells me she's a good-natured human. Her brown eyes appear hypnotized. Desmon's presence seems to have disabled her senses. I'm glad the people who have been around me these last few days never seemed to be this affected by my presence. Perhaps my human side is a blessing.

Desmon removes his cap, revealing thick brown hair. A few strands hang over his eyes. He bends next to the bed and looks at me. "You know what irritates me more than anything?"

I shake my head, dread rising within me.

He laughs. "You are the only person who doesn't bend to my will. I've come across so many different types of people in this world, supernatural and human, and all of them do exactly what I tell them, but you…" he points his finger at me, "you don't, and I'm beginning to find it rather exhausting."

Desmon walks to the edge of the bed. "At first, it was a challenge. You lied to me and that intrigued me, but now…the openly belligerent refusal to do what I ask of you…to ignore your nature and refuse to feed to feel better. I don't understand it at all."

"I'm not like you."

"No, you're not. I thought you were and we could get along splendidly, but your make-up is all wrong. How can you possibly have feelings for these creatures?" He points to the girl. Desmon goes around to the other side of the bed, facing her. Her head turns with his every movement.

"Don't, please, Desmon." Tears fall again, but I hold in my discomfort as best I can. "It doesn't have to be this way."

Desmon jumps on the bed, right on top of the girl, staring down at her. She reaches for him. He bends, kissing her on the mouth, and slides down to her neck, while watching me. She moans, as he thrusts his clothed body downward.

"No, please, Desmon," I beg him. "Let her go."

"Your whining is exhausting to listen to." He squeezes her further into the bedcovers. "I thought it would be fun to see you take a human life...to see the effect it has on you."

Desmon rolls off her and stands next to the bed, looking down at her. He shrugs and looks at the girl. "Stand up."

She stands beside him, gazing into his eyes, a smile plastered on her face.

"Since you won't take her, I will."

"Desmon, please don't do this," I implore him one more time.

"Ellie, get your emotions in check and let your nature take control." He grabs the girl's ass, licking his lips.

"Oh God! Oh God! Oh God!" I struggle with the ropes binding my hands and feet. It's no use. I'm weak, having had no food or water in more than a day. There's an awful sinking feeling in my stomach.

"Kiss me," Desmon says to her in a seductive voice, a different voice from the one he's been using. It's as if he's two dissimilar people. Their kiss sounds sloppy. I wonder if he's kissing her loudly on purpose or if he's that lousy of a kisser to begin with.

Then the moans starts: it's her moaning, and boisterously. It's as if all of her self-control has evaporated and she doesn't even remember I'm in the room. She wraps her arms around him and lifts one leg, trying to straddle him. My stomach twists; I want to hurl, but there's nothing in my stomach to throw-up.

As quickly as it started, the moaning slows. She emits a slight scream, but it fades to a gasp. She's struggling for her life now. I know that sound from the woods. Shawn made that noise as his life left him. He knew the end was coming and he struggled, but it was too late. Instead of holding him, she's attempting to push him away. She realizes her life is in danger.

"No! Please stop!" I plea, hoping Desmon will understand mercy.

And then…silence. No more struggling. It's as noiseless as a cold winter night when everybody is locked away inside their warm houses. I steal a moment of silence among the snow-covered woods with the trees as my only companions and pray for this girl I never knew.

Her lifeless body falls to the ground, pale and sallow looking.

"Des—" I cry. I cry for the nameless girl lying dead on the floor, who will never see her parents or friends again, who gave her life to this monster.

"Yes?" Desmon smiles. His aura flashes a bright, fluorescent green and fades to a dark mass of grass-colored greed.

"Why?" I ask through the tears. Tears I am getting used to shedding these last two days.

Desmon breathes in deeply and exhales, closing his eyes. "It's blissfully satisfying." He jumps onto the bed and lays beside me, facing me. He brushes away my tears. "You're all puffy when you're upset, you know."

"Why are you so evil?"

"Who's to say I'm evil? Maybe I'm an angel bringing an idyllically merciful death to these miserable people. Look at how some of them live. They are in pain most of the time, and I merely take that pain away."

I shake my head. "This is about your *pleasure*, not their pain."

He places his head on his arms and stares into my eyes. "You have a rather sadistic view of our kind. This is what we do. You've done it. Your mother's done it. It's for our survival. I don't get you. I don't understand this emotional mess that makes you up. Why are you being a hypocrite? I know you fed recently. Your mother must need to feed often, as well. Over the past three hundred years, I've needed it more and more."

He twists his head and moves closer to my face.

"You're wrong. Mother hasn't fed in more than twenty-three years and the only reason I did was to save a friend's life. You'll never understand the way I think because you don't have a heart."

"Twenty-three years, huh? I think you're mistaken. There's no way she could go that long without the energy. And, you're wrong, my dear." He smiles. "I have a heart, as do all of our kind. Kiss me."

"What?"

"I want you to kiss me," he scoots an inch away from me.

"Never!" Desmon's fist pummels down so fast, I

Hearts Aligning

barely close my eye before it hits me.

Chapter Twenty-Two
Day Seven (Halloween)

It's Halloween. I hadn't realized it until now, as the sun sets and the evening grows darker. It's the last day the portals will be open, and Mother may never get to go home now.

My face aches. The area around my right eye is swollen.

"I've got another surprise for you." Desmon walks into the room, but I keep my gaze fixed on the window. My stomach tightens at the sound of his voice. "Don't you want to know what it is?"

"No. Your surprises are meant to hurt me."

He unties my feet. I look down toward the edge of the bed. "You, Ellie, only hurt yourself. I've tried to be nice over and over again, but you, always the negative, solemn hybrid twist the meaning of my surprises."

"If your surprise doesn't consist of letting me go free, then I want to hear nothing about it." I close my eyes, wondering if I've struck his bad side once more. He's a ticking time bomb, waiting to go off at any moment.

Desmon places a gun on the nightstand next to the bed. I tense. How much longer will I live? Why doesn't he suck the life out of me? A bullet sounds much less painful than the withering away of my body. It should be quick. For once, a firearm seems like a better option.

Desmon yanks the ropes from the headboard to the bed and pulls my hands down in front of me. "Get up. It's time to take a little walk." My feet land on soft cream carpet, but fail to balance me as I'm shoved forward. He grabs the gun and sticks it against my back. This is the first time anyone has ever pointed a gun at me, and it's not a pleasant feeling.

Desmon holds the gun in his right hand and the excess rope connected to my hands in the other. The poor dead girl lays on the ground, her mouth open and her hollow eyes stare at nothing. Goosebumps form all over my arms. I step over her and out of the room.

"Where are we going?" I ask, as he leads me through the hall. I peer into the next room and see a stack of bodies. That explains the odor permeating through the vents. I close my eyes, hoping their deaths brought them peace, but knowing it was too soon for any of them to go. The guilt of taking Shawn's life surfaces once more. He wasn't a great guy, and he was about to kill my friend, but I think there could have been another way.

"We are going to Asteria," Desmon says. "Isn't

that where you wanted to go?"

He leads me through the foyer and points to the side table. A stone sits in a basket. It's the stone I'd been searching for, the one we need to get to Asteria. The blue is magnificent, with gold streaks throughout and black flakes swirling within the other colors. It's perfectly round and the size of a softball; so much larger than I had expected.

"Take it," Desmon says. I scoop it up into my bound hands.

He smiles at me and my stomach churns. "It's spectacular, isn't it?"

Desmon opens the front door and pulls me across the threshold. Not bothering to close the door, he drags me around the front of the house to the street. The neighborhood appears abandoned, and I realize I'm not far from town. Many of my old schoolmates lived here. The high school and cemetery aren't far, a tad to the south. He drags me east to the woods.

"Where are we going?" I ask.

"To a portal I've been watching all week. The wolves don't monitor it as they do most of the others, and few creatures have emerged from it. It should be safe enough, even for tonight." He looks up into the tall treetops as he pulls me into the woods.

"How will you get to Asteria?" I imagine he has a plan I haven't been privy to. "It's getting late."

The sun sets and the moon becomes the only light in the woods. Small beams of moonlight stream through the few patches the leaves don't cover. Soon, the winter months will come and all of the leaves will have fallen off these trees, but I may not be alive to see it.

Desmon smiles. "Your mother is meeting us, I'm sure. Unless you don't matter to her, that is."

I try to keep my voice calm, as a new terror overcomes me. "What makes you think she will be there?"

"Do you think she'd allow you to die?" Desmon doesn't elaborate. The thought of my imminent demise makes me shiver.

"Why don't you stay here where you're so rich and powerful?" The thought of this crazed lunatic going to a once peaceful plane doesn't sound like it would benefit the people there at all.

"The thought crossed my mind, and for a while I thought I'd have no choice, but you've convinced me it's the best option."

"I did?" What could I possibly have said that convinced him to want to leave? He's the one who complained about how Asteria wasn't the peaceful place I'd imagined and how he was a 'God' here.

"Seeing how you act around these humans nauseates me. Perhaps it's because you're half human, but when you said your mother hadn't fed in a while, it made me think that eventually my boredom will increase. I don't want to be stuck here if I might lose interest in feeding, as well. I'm feeling bored now, actually."

"Are you going to kill us?"

"The thought has crossed my mind. I certainly can't have your mother go back to Asteria with me;

she'd more than likely take control."

Anger boils within me. "You'd better not hurt her. I don't care what you do to me, but leave her alone!"

"If she brings the staff, as she's supposed to, and doesn't interfere, then I'll let her live out her useless life here." He stops and pulls me close, putting his mouth to my ear. "And, only if you agree to come with me, and submit to me."

"Why? Why would you want that?" I cringe at his touch.

"Have you ever heard of that old saying 'you want what you can't have'? Well, you, Ellie, are my challenge. You've denied me and I won't have that."

He's not used to being rejected, that's obvious.

"Don't do this," I beg. "You don't want me. I'm half human and I don't belong there."

It had been a dream of mine to go to Asteria with my mother, but now all I want to do is stay here, away from him, and with Bryan and Faith and Mom.

"You're the one who wanted to see Asteria in all its glory." He continues walking, pulling me along like a dog. "Remember? That peaceful place that is perfection."

"You're the one who told me it wasn't perfect."

"Lily was right about a lot of things. It's much more peaceful than here, but it still had its own unbearable political system. It's time for the royal family to be usurped. It's time for change in Asteria, and I'm the one to bring it."

We walk in silence. Several wolves howl in the

distance. Desmon stops for a moment, and then continues through the dark woods. The air feels heavy. The moon appears much closer to Earth than usual. Glass shatters in the distance, evidence we aren't far from town. It seems the other residents are experiencing more upheaval tonight. I pray Bryan and Faith are safe in the bar, and it hasn't been damaged any further.

The bar—I'm a horrible person. I didn't have a will made up. I feel so unprepared and now I can't even show my loved ones I care, even in death. I would have left it to Faith. She could have inherited all that I would have, and been able to care for herself.

Regrets swarm my mind. Grandpa left journals for me and they provided a great deal of comfort, but I have left nothing behind. I should have told Bryan he's made this past week one of the best of my life. I should have thanked Faith for all those wonderful years of friendship. I should have told Eddie how much I appreciated him being there for me after my grandfather passed…Eddie, whom I'll never see again, because of this pig before me.

It's funny how certain thoughts plague me now that I think my end may be near. There's no way in hell I'll agree to submit to Desmon. I'd rather die than agree to his terms, but I have to save my mother. Once we are through the portal he can't harm her and I'll find a way to make him end me.

Desmon stops in front of a tree with a ladder leaning against it. I look up and see the hunting blind that sits on a large tree limb. It's a place where hunters sit and wait for deer.

"Go up, now." Desmon pushes me to the ladder.

I hold up my hands. "It's not going to be easy climbing with my hands tied and a large stone in between them."

Desmon grabs the stone from me and shoves it into a large pocket on his cargo pants. "Do it." He nudges me upward.

Taking my time, I position myself steady on the first rung and use my body weight to lift myself onto the ladder. Carefully, and leaning into it, I take one step at a time and use my hands together as best I can. It seems like it takes an hour for me to get to the platform, but I eventually make it, Desmon right on my tail.

The blind covers the platform, but there are many supplies here. I can tell Desmon has been here before since he moves straight to the edge and grabs a pair of binoculars. They must be night vision, because I don't know how else he can actually see through them.

He stares toward a section of the blackened woods.

"Where is the portal?"

He doesn't answer me.

A scream in the distance makes me jump. It's coming from town, and we can't be far from it, maybe a few hundred feet directly east. "Jesus Christ!"

"All this time, they've left the portal alone and

now they choose to guard it?" Desmon turns to me. "Those wolves had better be gone when your mother shows up, or she's not following my instructions."

Wolves…Bryan. One of them has to be Bryan.

He takes a rifle from the platform and points it in the darkness, near where he was looking.

"What are you doing?"

"Maybe it'll be easier to take them out now and be done with it." Desmon peers through the scope.

"That'll draw more attention from the others and they'll come searching for you."

He puts the rifle down and looks at me. "Why, Ellie, are you trying to help us or the wretched werewolves?"

"No one needs to get hurt. Give it some time until she gets here."

Leave wolves, leave, I plead silently.

Desmon sits next to the rifle and pulls on the rope so hard that I tumble into his lap. "How shall we pass the time?"

I try to push away, but the rope's shortened grip doesn't allow me to move far.

"How about a little affection?" Desmon asks. "Maybe a show of effort on your part to save your mother's life? Wouldn't it be splendid to see her live through this?" He raises his right eyebrow, waiting for my answer.

Chapter Twenty-Three
Day Seven (Halloween)

The memory of Desmon's fist hitting my face settles on repeat in my head, as he brushes the hair from my face.

Desmon sighs. "It'll be so nice to get you all cleaned up and pretty, don't you think? To see you in a nice gown, covered in sheer lace and pearls. Yes, you'll do nicely by my side."

I say nothing for fear of awakening his anger and madness. At times, Desmon seems normal, with a pleasant voice, but then he'll snap and become the madman again. Why must he be so affectionate toward me? Is it truly because I'm the only one who has rejected him?

Desmon ticks his tongue again. "I see it in your eyes. Your contempt isn't well hidden and you are no longer drawn to me like that night you ran out in front of my car."

He pushes me away, thank goodness.

Desmon's right. That feeling of shared kinship has disappeared and I hadn't noticed. Only loathing and hatred emerge when he's near me. There's no draw to him, no connection. I've severed that, somehow.

"You have nothing to say?" I shake my head. "Do you know why this is?" I shake my head again. "It's your human side, obviously. I'm still drawn to you. It's practically electric, but you aren't experiencing it any longer. I see it in your aura, your movement and expressions. It's irritating, but you'll have to change this if you want to live. You need to figure out how to bring the succubus out again, or you won't fit in at home."

"Asteria isn't my home." I look at the ground, not wanting to make eye contact any more than necessary. I think about the place I was so excited to see only days before, but now I realize the truth—I don't belong there. With Desmon there, it would be a prison.

"Oh, but it is." Desmon looks through the binoculars again, and then at his watch. I lean against the wooden boards, close my eyes, and pray that Mother doesn't show up. If she keeps the staff away until past midnight, then Desmon's chance to take me away will be gone and he'll be stuck here, preying on others for centuries to come. I can't clear my head long enough to figure out what the best scenario would be. If he's stuck here, likely he'll kill me and many others; but if he leaves, he might kill there as well. Who's to say what he'll do?

I try to banish these horrid thoughts and think about the one night with Bryan in the woods on the way to Mother's cabin, where we shared my bed. How did I find bliss during this nightmare in Saint's Grove? Even if it were for such a brief time, I was happy. I hope Bryan stays on his positive course in life, even if I'm not in it. Maybe he will start to sketch again or contact his brother and mend those fences.

Hours pass in silence. The night noises become my companion, and the good memories my savior. I've made peace with whatever the outcome will be, which will most likely end in my death.

"It's time." Desmon yanks me from my reverie. "Let's go."

Desmon's disposition has changed, and I'm thankful. He's not smiling. He's brooding. I can sense that in his putrid aura. Desmon checks the gun and makes sure the bullet is loaded in the chamber. He pats his pants to be certain the stone is still in his pocket, and points to the ladder.

I guess I'm going first. I turn around and crawl backwards across a few boards until my foot feels the first rung. He watches me as I descend, holding the rope that's tied to my hands. Once I get to the middle, he turns and follows.

"Where are we going?" I ask, once he's on the ground.

"That way." Desmon points with the gun. He wants me to take the lead. I walk in the direction he motioned to, the moonlight my only guide through the dark forest.

Every few minutes, Desmon redirects me onto the

right path. It feels as if we have walked for a good 15 minutes before I see the fog. A loud flapping sound causes us both to look up. The shadow of a large dragon-like creature flies over the treetops. I'm afraid to see the portal that it came through. We continue walking into the murkiness of the night.

Fog covers the ground by the portal. I look closely at it, wondering if something strange will emerge and become trapped in our world. Maybe something will come out and eat Desmon—that would certainly make my night better.

As we grow closer, I notice a dark figure standing to the west of the portal and my heartbeat quickens. Mother's wearing her cloak and looks so menacing in the night.

"I can't see you," Desmon says to the dark shadow. "Your aura's missing, and that must be why you've been so successful at hiding from the world, isn't it Lily?"

She removes her hood, revealing her fake older face.

"Well, the years haven't been as kind to you as they have to me, have they?"

Desmon pulls me to a stop 15 feet from Mother. "Take it off, Lily, and let me see your aura," he demands, holding the gun against my back.

She removes the cloak and lets it drop to the ground. Her green aura mixes with the fog and the moonlight, and her appearance changes. She holds the staff, previously hidden under her cloak, in her left hand for him to see.

"That's better, but I do see you aging. Don't you have anything to say?"

"Let my daughter go and you can have the staff."

"Lily, after all these years. How did you survive this brutal world and that even more vicious night?"

"Father saved me. He died protecting me from the monsters that killed everyone else, and you should have been among those bodies."

"I see where you get your horrid attitude, Ellie."

"You hurt her." Mom looks at my face.

"We've had some rather unfortunate interactions. I see you've brought the staff, but you didn't come alone."

Two pair of yellow eyes stare at us through the veil of darkness, one in the east, the other in the west. Faith steps out of the shadows, joining Mother. The unusual angry look on her face is an expression I've never seen before. She's pissed.

"Take it, let her go, and leave," Mother says, holding the staff out toward us.

"You've put me in a awkward position, Lily." Desmon watches the yellow eyes as they blink in the night. "If I let Ellie go, your friends will rip me to pieces, won't they?"

"Would you blame them?" Mother asks. "You killed a close friend of theirs and left a note on his body. There was no way I could be discreet about our meeting."

"I'm so sorry," I tell the wolves. I know one is Bryan, but it's too dark to tell where he is. I turn to Faith and mouth *I'm sorry* to her, too.

Desmon yanks me back. A growl erupts from the east.

"I guess we will have to do this differently than I planned. Do your hounds care anything for your daughter?" Desmon looks at the wolf that growled when he pulled me. He moves the gun from my back and places it against my head.

"Stop!" Mom yells. "Put the gun down. They won't harm you if you let her go. You have my word."

Faith steps forward and raises her hands.

"I'd stop that little witch if I were you. I can pull this trigger faster than she can finish that spell." Desmon pulls me closer.

Faith lowers her arms and bites her lip.

"The word of a succubus here means nothing to me. You've been among these humans far too long; I'm sure you're more like them than like us." Desmon purses his lips. "Back up, you mutts!" He turns, placing his back to the portal and shielding himself with me in front of him.

"Oh, God!" I cry.

"Lily, bring the staff to us, slowly, and give it to your daughter." Desmon pulls the stone out of his pocket with his free hand and holds it out.

"Let her go and you'll get the staff," Mother says.

"No! This is not a bargaining session. Give Ellie the damned staff or I'll shoot her and neither of us will leave happy." His voice rises in frustration. "Do it now!"

Desmon looks at his watch for a second. I know

time is running out, along with his patience.

"Okay, okay." Mom slowly walks the few feet toward me, but the wolf to her left leaps in front of Mom, preventing her from bringing me the staff.

Desmon moves the gun from my head and aims it at the wolf.

"No!" I yell, but it's too late, the gun fires before I shove him back.

Another wolf rushes from the woods like a lightning bolt, striking so quickly that before I can turn my head a massive, furry lump squashes my mother. The bullet hits one of the wolves, but I'm not sure which.

"Stay back." Desmon aims the gun at the wolf left standing next to my mother. It growls and backs away, shaking.

The wolves change into two naked men—Bryan, and Mitch, his father. Bryan leans over his father, who lies on the ground, blood pooling underneath him. The bullet went through his chest. Bryan covers the wound with his hand, and tears fall from his face.

I can't take my gaze from son and father. Bryan's trembling and speaking to his father, but I can't make out the words.

"What have you done?" My limbs shake and an ache forms in my center.

"The staff, Lily, or the next bullet is Ellie's." Desmon eases back, pulling me along. "Throw it now!"

Mom retrieves the staff, watching Bryan and Mitch on the ground. She turns to me; her aura screams desperation and panic. She tosses the staff and it lands in front of my feet.

I pick it up. Desmon places the stone atop the staff, where it immediately attaches itself, as if magnetically reuniting two artifacts that belong together.

"Place it in front of the portal, in the moonlight," Desmon says.

Mom's dreadful expression scares me. She widens her eyes and looks down at the staff. I try to follow her gaze. Her expression is telling me something, but I don't know what.

I turn west and raise the staff to the moonlight, but I need to raise it higher because it's too short to hit the stream of light correctly.

"Hurry," Desmon growls.

"I'm trying." I inch the staff up with my bound hands, enough that it finally hits the moonlight, and that's when I feel it—a button on the staff.

The light shines through the stone and into the portal, opening it up to another world—Asteria.

Desmon turns to see it.

Mom looks at me and the staff once more; her eyes seem erratic. I press the button and the bottom of the staff falls free, revealing the shiniest of objects...a knife.

Desmon pulls me toward the portal. "Let's go, now."

"No!" Mother yells.

Bryan jumps up, removing his hand from his father's wound, ready to take on another bullet.

Desmon shakes his head, yanks me away, and points the gun at Bryan.

"The staff!" Mother yells.

I push the staff up as high as I can with my bound hands and bring it around my side, then thrust the sharp edge into Desmon's chest with as much strength as I have.

Desmon falls back. The gun tilts up and fires into the night sky. It tumbles from his hand as he reaches for the knife lodged deep inside him. His eyes widen, and blood spills out of his mouth.

Chapter Twenty-Four
Day Seven (Halloween)

I cover my mouth with my bound hands, quivering uncontrollably. Desmon's dead eyes remain fixed on me as his last breath leaves his body.

Someone pulls me away from the portal entrance...Bryan. He cups my face, shielding me away from Desmon's body.

"You're okay," he says.

I nod. Bryan quickly kisses me. He turns to his dad lying against the nearest tree trunk.

"Go!" I urge him. Faith and Mom rush to me. I see tears streaming down Faith's cheeks. Mom unbinds my ropes. Bryan bends next to his father.

"Faith, go for help." I watch Mitch's helpless form on the ground. She squeezes me tightly, nods, and rushes back to town.

Having untied me, Mom turns to Bryan and Mitch. Mitch holds up a blood-soaked hand and shakes his head. He doesn't speak.

"Dad, you can make it," Bryan says.

Mitch brings his hand up to Bryan's face and shakes his head slowly again.

"No! Dammit! No!" Bryan shouts.

Mitch pulls Bryan's head close to him, whispering into his ear. His arms drop to the ground on his last breath.

Bryan cries out and beats his fist against his father's dead chest. I drop down next to him, wrapping my arms around him. He turns and squeezes me so tightly, burrowing his head into my shoulder.

"Ellie…" Mom's voice sounds so distant.

Bryan pulls away and wipes his face with his dirty hands, leaving a trail of blood and dirt down the right side of his face. He stands and pulls me up with him.

"Ellie, it's time to go." Mom gazes at the open portal to Asteria. In the distant background I see a bright rolling hill covered with tall grass.

Bryan grabs my hand and squeezes.

Mom looks at her watch. "The portal will close in two minutes. This will be our only chance to go home." She steps on Desmon's chest and pulls the staff free; the stone stays attached to it.

"If you want to go, I won't stop you," Bryan says to me. "But, my home is here. My mom will need me now more than ever."

He looks at Mitch's motionless body, then leans into me and whispers, "But I don't want you to leave me. I'm in love with you."

I turn to Mother. "Stay with us! This is my

home."

She rushes toward me. "I know this is your home. You have friends here that have become your family, more than I've ever been." Mother turns toward the portal. "But, I don't belong here. This isn't my home, and the only time I felt at peace here was with your father. But that time is over; I have to go. The cravings…are becoming too unbearable and I don't want to end up like him." She looks at Desmon's body.

Bryan releases my hand. I hug my mother.

"I love you, Ellie, and I want you to be happy here forever and always." My mother kisses my cheek. "Take care of your friends and know that happiness is what you make it. It's not defined by a place or a time, but by the people you surround yourself with."

"I only just found you." Tears roll down my eyes, and an emptiness forms in my stomach.

She takes my face in her hands. "I've always been here." She points to my heart. "And so has your father."

I nod.

"Take care of her," she says to Bryan.

Mother grabs the staff and disappears through the portal. The stone rolls back out onto the foggy ground, landing at my feet, and the portal disappears.

Howls erupt in the distance, surrounding us.

"It's midnight." Bryan looks up at the sky.

I pick the stone up and hold it between my sore hands.

Bryan wraps his arms around me from behind. "You stayed."

I face him. "Of course, I stayed. My home is here, with you."

He hugs me and we remain entwined for several minutes. Our stress melts away but a cloud of despair remains. My mind races through the events of the evening. We both lost a parent tonight; parents from whom we were estranged before this week, but who had shown us how deeply they cared.

"Thank you," he whispers in my ear.

"For what?"

"For staying and choosing to be a part of my life."

"I love you, Bryan." The words feel natural, right, and it's the first time I've said them to a man other than my grandfather.

He backs away, places his hands on my cheeks and looks into my eyes. "I love you more than I can possibly express with words."

Epilogue
Day Sixty-One (December 24th)

"Are we closing at seven?" Faith loads glasses into the tub to be washed in the back.

I nod as I wipe down the bar. "You bet. Most of the stores are closing at six, so we can kick the stragglers out by then."

It's after lunch hour and a few tables are full, packages surrounding everyone's chairs. They are more into the food today than the beer.

"Order up!" Russell rings the bell. He loves ringing that stupid bell.

"You don't have to ring the bell when we're standing two feet apart, Russ." I smile and take the plates through the open kitchen counter.

"Oh, I know." He winks at Faith, who turns crimson.

Russell turns back to the grill. I take the food to the hungry patrons. When I return, I see Bryan coming into the bar with his mother. He smiles and leads her to the table by the new bay window. It had to be replaced after Halloween. The original was smashed to pieces by what Faith called a primate-looking cave dweller with a rather large pointy tail. Can't say I'm upset with not seeing that one.

"Isn't he cute?" Faith asks.

"Yes." I nod, gawking at Bryan.

"Not him, you lovesick puppy." Faith swats me with a towel. "I mean Russell."

I turn to see her smiling at Russell through the window. I think I hired him intentionally because she drooled when he came in for an interview.

I laugh.

Then, the door opens again and my lawyer walks in. He nods and comes to the bar. "I'm here, as requested." Mr. Woodward doesn't look happy about meeting me on Christmas Eve. "I have the papers."

He pulls them out of his briefcase, and he follows me to an empty table.

"Are you sure you want to do this, Ms. Whitaker?" He asks, as we sit across from each other.

"Absolutely."

Two new patrons enter the bar and Bryan rushes to one of them—his brother. He grabs him in a massive bear hug and turns him in a circle. His mother joins the embrace and it's one of the sweetest things to witness. Everyone in the bar quiets and watches for that moment, before returning to their meals.

"Okay, where is the lucky girl?" Mr. Woodward asks.

I turn toward the bar. "Faith, come here a moment

please."

Faith walks over, grimacing. She's been pestering me about selling the bar, lately. She thinks Bryan and I will be going on a world trip and leave her alone here in Saint's Grove.

"Yes, Master," she says with a theatrical bow. "Can I get you something, Master?"

"You can sit down and sign these damn papers Mr. Woodward has brought."

"What?"

"Ms. Whitaker is making you a partner in the bar." Mr. Woodward smiles.

"What?" Faith asks again, turning to me.

"Merry Christmas, Faith," I say, and she jumps up and down, covering her mouth, her newly-dyed purple, curly hair flying in all directions.

I stand and hug her, making us the center of attention for a moment.

Bryan smiles at me from across the room. He knew what I had planned. His brother and mother sit beside him; his mother holds Rob's hand and pats him on the cheek.

A customer walks to the register and I excuse myself to take care of the patron.

"Was everything okay?" I ask the customer.

"Absolutely." He pays the bill and walks out with his multiple bags.

I stand at the counter, watching Faith sign the papers, a smile plastered on her face.

"Hey!" A new face stands in front of me. It's Bryan's brother. "I want to introduce myself. I'm

Rob." Bryan stands next to him, beaming. It's that award-winning smile from high school once again.

"Hi, I'm Ellie," I scoot around the bar to hug him. "It's so nice to finally meet you."

"You, too. You look exactly like your drawing."

"Drawing?" I ask. "What drawing?"

Rob pulls out his wallet and unfolds a sketch of me.

"Oh." I take it and see my face perfectly drawn in pencil. I'm overwhelmed. I've never seen my portrait before.

"Amazing, huh? He's talented, and I'm so glad he's drawing again." Rob grabs Bryan around the shoulders and tugs him into a side hug.

"Extremely talented," I say.

"All right, that's enough." Bryan pushes him away playfully. Rob returns to his mother and boyfriend who eagerly awaits them at their table.

I look up at Bryan, and we both smile. "I didn't know you started sketching again."

He pulls me into a loving embrace. "I have inspiration again, and she drives me crazy."

"Good crazy, I hope?"

He bends and kisses me. "The best kind of crazy."

Yes, I've found my home and happiness, and it's right here in Saint's Grove.

Acknowledgements

Hearts Aligning has been an incredible book to write, consisting of countless hours of writing, research, and brainstorming with the other wonderful Saint's Grove authors, but wouldn't have arrived without the help from many other wonderful people as well.

I'd like to first thank my family, who has allowed me to spend valuable time outside of my regular responsibilities in order to pursue my passions. I love you all very much.

I'd like to thank my editor, Todd Barselow, who helped shape this exciting story.

I'd like to thank my friend, and second editor, Keith B. Darrell. You are an inspiration to me and I hope to have half your talent one day.

A special thanks to Najla Qamber, who is the wonderful and amazing cover designer. Not only is her work fantastic, but she goes beyond to bring my vision alive.

This story has become stronger with the help of my gracious and fabulous beta readers and critique partners. Thank you to Eimy Socas, Carly Fall, and Ainsley Shay. You mean so much to me, and I couldn't have done this without you.

Finally, I'd like to thank the readers who honor me by reading *Hearts Aligning*. Thank you! Thank you! Thank you!

About the Author

Miranda Hardy writes children's, young adult and new adult literature to keep the voices in her head appeased. When she's not in her fantasy worlds, she's canoeing in alligator infested waters, or rescuing homeless animals. She goes to coffee shops to do most of her writing while drinking tea. Unable to reveal too much, she has the most boring superpower ever (hint: you have to be a close relative for it to work). She resides in south Florida with her two wonderful children, and too many animals to mention.

Centuries ago, she was a princess and he a knight. Their forbidden love was torn apart by circumstances of the times, and her brutal death...

Arabella "Bella" Franklin has a nice, stable life in Saint's Grove, Virginia. With no recollection of her previous existence as a princess, the newly-reincarnated young woman is living the dream—a successful bakery owner with some semblance of a social life. However, boredom and loneliness continue to be her constant companions.

Those feelings quickly disappear when the townspeople gather to witness a once-in-a-lifetime, major astrological event. Unbeknownst to them, the occurrence opens the seams of the universe, allowing any and all paranormal entities to descend onto the quiet town, transforming it into a place of mayhem and danger.

When Bella is attacked by a vicious demon, Jayden, an Angel of Death, comes to her rescue. Unlike Bella, he remembers everything about their past lives, and is delighted knowing that their reunion will give him an opportunity to possibly rekindle their passion, as well as regain his life as a human. But becoming human again comes with three caveats. He must convince Bella of the love they shared so many centuries ago, she must kill a demon – her murderer from her previous life – and she has to want Jayden to stay.

With only seven days to meet those demands, memories of her past life begin to surface. With them, comes the knowledge that if she can't kill the demon before the seal closes, she—and possibly Jayden—may be forced to spend eternity in Hell.

Read on for an excerpt from Her Forbidden Knight by Carly Fall!

Her Forbidden Knight

By

Carly Fall

"Her Forbidden Knight' is a work of fiction. Names, characters, places, and incidents either are the product of the author's imagination or are used FICTITIOUSLY. Any resemblance to actual persons, living or dead, events or locales is purely coincidental."

Chapter 2

Arabella Franklin stood behind the counter of her bakery, Bella's Bake Shop, known by the town residents of Saint's Grove, Virginia as 'Bella's'—which was fine with her. She appreciated that everyone shortened her name. Before retiring, her mother had taught fourteenth century history at the local community college, and had given her a name popular during the medieval times. Frankly, she hated it, and used the abbreviated version whenever possible.

The sun would be setting soon, and she had

decided to stay open late tonight since almost the whole population of Saint's Grove would gather in the town's square for the astronomical event. The planets Earth, Mars, Venus, Jupiter, Saturn, and Mercury would line up perfectly at the same time as a total lunar eclipse. The astrology professor at the community college stated that an event like this would most likely never happen again in their lifetimes…if ever again.

The City Council had decided to make a big party out of the event. Families would gather, blankets would be laid out on the lawn, and the mayor, Thomas Barlow—who had an uncanny resemblance to Hugh Jackman—even planned to give a little speech. The astrology professor would be present to answer any questions, and Bella hoped people would also want some of her cookies and cupcakes.

Being the only baker in town, she kept busy with weddings, birthdays, holidays, and even a funeral every now and then. With her shop situated in the town square, the morning crowd loved to come in for a cup of coffee and one of her freshly made muffins before heading off to their own jobs. The hair salon next door also provided a steady stream of customers looking for their afternoon sugar fix. Overall, business was good.

A woman who frequented her store in the mornings came in with a little girl in tow, and smiled at Bella.

"I'm so glad you stayed open," the woman beamed. "The kids are dying for some of your chocolate chip cookies."

Bella grinned at the little girl, whose hair hung

around her face in messy, blonde corkscrew curls.

"Great! How many?"

The little girl jumped up and down. "Six!"

Her mother shook her head. "You aren't eating six cookies, Mary. We'll take four. That's one for you, one for your brother, and your dad and I will each have one."

"Mommy, can I have two?" the girl pleaded.

"No."

Bella met the mother's gaze, wishing she could remember the woman's name. She came into the store almost every morning, and Bella recalled she worked at the post office located kitty-corner from the bakery.

Reaching into the display case, she heard the bell ring, indicating she had more customers. She carefully removed four cookies and set them in a little blue box, then sealed it with a sticker carrying her business logo—a gold, foil circle embossed with the letter *B*.

The woman handed Bella a credit card, and she rang up the transaction.

"You're going to close pretty soon, right?" The woman asked excitedly. "You can't be working with this amazing event happening!"

Bella grinned. "I will. I wouldn't miss it."

"Good. Hopefully, we'll see you out there, Bella!"

The woman and her child left, and Sophia Rose Neilson, the manager of Saint's Grove Bank, stepped up to the counter. Bella had always liked the woman, as Sophia seemed to be one of those people who lit up a room whenever she entered. Her smart, blue eyes seemed to always gleam with happiness, and her long, dark hair always held glimpses of purple, similar to her own. The woman had been working at the bank for five years, and had actually given Bella her loan to get the bakery going. They chatted for a minute while Bella packed up two chocolate chip muffins, and then Sophia left. A steady stream of customers kept her busy for another hour.

By the time she thought to glance outside again, darkness had descended. She wished she had time to tidy up the store, but then came to the conclusion she'd stay a bit late tonight, or come in earlier than usual in the morning.

She stepped out into the cool night air and locked the door, deciding she'd love a cocktail. Walking across the square, she headed for the bar and grill. She heard the murmurs that the six planets had lined up in the sky, and she glanced upward. Six lights shone, all aligned together. She had also heard the astronomy professor had brought his telescope for those who wanted a closer look. Maybe she'd try to find him after visiting the bar.

Stepping into the Mountaintop Bar and Grill, she nodded at the owner, Genevieve Eleanor Whitaker, who went by Ellie. She stood behind the bar wiping down the wooden surface, her brunette hair in the usual ponytail, her milky skin glowing under the lights. The place was pretty empty since everyone was gathered outside.

Ellie gave her a wave. "Hey, Bella. Are you open tonight?"

She nodded. "I was. What about you? Have you been busy?"

"A bit. What can I get for you?"

Bella leaned over the bar so that the few other patrons wouldn't hear her. "Vodka and tonic. Can I get it in a to-go cup? I'm going back to the store in a little bit to clean up."

Ellie smiled. "You got it."

It was illegal to have alcohol outside of a drinking establishment, but she felt certain there had to be a few hidden flasks among the crowd out there. She just wanted to enjoy her drink without any hassle.

They chatted a few more minutes. Bella threw a few bills on the bar and then headed back to the bakery.

Standing in the doorway of her store, she took in all the families, heard the chatter and laughter, and center of her chest ached.

At age thirty, she knew she missed something in her life, but couldn't figure out what exactly it could be. If you'd asked her ten years ago to imagine her life at this time, she'd have said without hesitation that she'd be married with a couple of kids. She sighed at how wrong she'd been.

Her parents lived down the mountain in Roanoke, and she saw them a couple of times a month. Bella's Bake Shop did well, and many people relied on her to help them make their holidays and special occasions extraordinary; which meant she didn't get a lot of time to go out. Most of her friends were married with kids, so she didn't see much of them. She dated every now and then, but found that most men didn't interest her much.

Despite being busy, the feeling of emptiness only intensified with each day. If her life was missing something—or someone—it seemed to her she'd have to be aware of them. You couldn't long for anything you didn't know about. If you'd never known it before, how could it be missed?

Yet, she woke each morning feeling as though a part of her had disappeared. She didn't understand it. She'd fallen into a huge rut, one she couldn't climb out of. In a nutshell, her life bored her to tears, and she had no idea what to do about it.

As some of the kids ran around playing tag, she smiled. She would like to have children at some point, but in order to do that the old-fashioned way, she'd have to find a man. She didn't subscribe to the notion that a woman "needed" a man to feel whole or complete, though. Perhaps she should consider adoption instead.

What could be her unnamable need? Could it be all she required was a trip to a therapist and some anti-depressants? Was it that simple?

The sounds of "oohs" and "ahs" returned her to the present, and she noticed that many people were looking upward. She followed everyone's gaze, the crowd's excitement almost causing friction in the air. The night had come alive with what she assumed to be a meteor shower. Bright, multi-colored lights zipped across the sky, as if it rained stars. It looked like they would land right on top of them, but it seemed like they somehow avoided the town square.

A moment later, an ear-piercing scream sounded from the front of the square, near the statue of the town's founder, Peter Saint. She moved out of the doorway to try seeing what had happened, but couldn't see past the throngs of people. Someone else yelled, and suddenly, all-out chaos ensued. A father picked up his son, grabbed his wife's hand, and began running away from the square, his face a mask of terror. Another woman ran past Bella, carrying her two children, as tears streamed down her face. Confusion tore through her as people scattered in all directions, and she looked again to see what had caused the mayhem, but then someone jostled her back into the doorway of her store.

People began to act panicked, but also strange. A pale man took down a running woman, then brought his mouth to her neck. At first, the woman screamed and thrashed, but a moment later, she lay limply in his arms. The man glanced up, not seeing Bella in the shadows. Blood dripped from his fangs and down his chin. He stood and seemed to disappear right before her eyes.

Okay, that apparently hadn't been a man, but a … *a vampire?*

Another woman ran up to her store, her long, black hair in disarray around her thin face. Bella dropped her cup as she stared into the woman's glowing, yellow eyes, fear coursing through her.

"Get inside," she hissed. "Keep the lights off."

Out of sheer terror, Bella did as instructed, unlocking the door with shaky hands. Once secured inside, she sat in the darkness, gazing out the window. The woman began to tremble and dropped to all fours. A second later, a large, black wolf stood in her place. Bella backed away from the door as a grey wolf ran at the black one. They tussled on the pavement for a moment, fangs flashing and deep growls emanating from both. Then, the black wolf took off with her attacker right behind her.

Bella's heart pounded in her chest and tears stung her eyes as she moved away from the door. Crouching down behind the counter, she watched the mêlée outside. Could she be in the middle of a nightmare? Had she lost her mind? Forget depression medicine. Right now, it seemed she needed to check into a psychiatric ward. She couldn't believe what she was seeing. Vampires? Werewolves?

A man ran toward her store, a look of terror painting his face. He stood about six-foot, rail thin, with thick black hair and a matching beard. His icy blue gaze grew wide as he looked around at the chaos surrounding him.

"Help me!" he screamed, pounding on her door.

She stood and studied him, fairly certain she hadn't seen him around town before, yet, a sense of familiarity overcame her.

"Please! Let me in! I'm going to die out here!"

Her gut told her not to trust him, but she couldn't turn her back on her fellow man, could she? Not with the chaos that had erupted so suddenly—not after what she'd just witnessed. The body of the woman who'd been attacked by the vampire lay on the street just mere feet away. The woman who had turned into a wolf had left her clothing strewn across her doorstep. This man begged for her to help him, to allow him into safety. She couldn't say no. Whatever had happened to cause this mayhem, the danger was very real.

Rounding the counter, she got halfway to the door and stopped. A man dressed in leather pants and vest descended from the sky, holding a long, silver sword and a matching knife. The black wings at his back spanned at least twelve feet from tip to tip. His dark hair tousled in the breeze. He hovered about ten feet behind the guy pounding on her door, his face a mask of dark rage.

She rubbed her eyes, hoping to clear what she saw. What was he? Some type of angel? Good angels wore white, right? Since he was dressed in black, did that make him … bad?

Rushing to the door, she opened it and let the man in.

"Oh, thank you. It's just terrifying out there."

Just as she tried to close the pane, the angel placed his foot in the doorway and shoved her backwards, trapping her between the glass door and the window.

"Don't move, Arabella," he snarled as his wings simply disappeared.

She stared at the space on his back where they'd been, then closed her eyes for a brief second, unable to believe what she'd just seen. It registered somewhere in the back of her mind that he knew her name, but she couldn't find the words to ask him how.

The man she'd tried to help suddenly morphed into what she could only describe as a demon. His hands changed into claws while his skin took on a red glow, and his eyes became two black orbs. Fangs protruded from his upper lip, and a forked tongue jutted from his mouth as he hissed at her savior.

Paralyzing fear tore through her, and she screamed as she pulled the door closer to her. She longed to shut her eyes, but found herself mesmerized.

The angel raised his sword. "This time, you will not succeed, Ulric."

The creature laughed, a deep, guttural sound that sent tremors of terror through her. "You failed once, Jayden, and you'll fail again—you won't be able to protect her. You're a pathetic excuse for a knight."

The angel, apparently named Jayden, lunged at the demon, his sword barely missing its head. Ulric dodged the blow, causing Jayden to go crashing into one of her display cases, then to the floor. The glass shattered and cupcakes flew around the store. Ulric pounced on him, and they traded blows. Jayden gained the upper hand and slammed the demon into the other display case, and it, too, met its demise. Ulric tried to get to his feet, but the smashed cakes made it difficult for him to keep his footing. Jayden grabbed a chair and raised it over his head. Just as he brought it down, the demon rolled away, sprang to his feet, and ran out the front door.

Bella stared after him, her whole body violently trembling, and the sound of splintering wood still echoing in her head from the crushed chair.

After a moment, she turned to Jayden. He looked at her, his chest heaving in labored breaths. Their gazes locked, and a feeling of recognition came over her. As she studied his dark eyes, high cheekbones, and square jaw, she tried to place from where she knew him. It was a ridiculous thought, because she didn't hang out with angels. In fact, she kept waiting to wake up safe in her own bed, relieved this evening had only been a horrible nightmare.

He stepped toward her as a trickle of fear clawed

down her spine, and she held on tightly to the door, the only barrier between them.

"I'm not going to hurt you, Arabella," Jayden reassured her.

She swallowed as tears clogged her throat. "My name's *Bella*."

Why she felt it important to correct him on her name, she didn't understand. She had just witnessed an epic battle between an angel and a demon. What he called her seemed irrelevant.

Then, she remembered her thought from earlier—how had he known her name?

She tried to speak, but the words remained caught within her throat.

Confusion crossed his face just for a second, but then disappeared as a gentle smile took its place. "Very well. I'm not here to harm you, Bella."

She glanced around her ruined store. If he'd wanted to hurt her, he already would have. Instead, he'd protected her from that ugly, awful, terrifying … thing.

"We should shut the door," he said softly. "The Evil is still out there. We don't want to invite it in."

It seemed like a rational thing to do, but she couldn't seem to let go of the pane. Her knuckles were white from holding on to the metal bar so tightly.

He came closer and placed his hand on the edge of the door. "Let me close this."

As he pulled, it slipped from her grasp. He turned the key in the lock, then glanced over at her. "I'm sorry about your bakery."

She really couldn't believe the mess. Smashed pastries and cakes littered the floor, topped with sprinklings of broken glass and splinters of wood. A little tidying up had turned into an epic clean up—almost a complete remodeling. At least the walls still stood.

He held his hand out to her. "Right now, this is the least of our worries."

She gazed up at him, and then back at his hand. Chaos continued outside, and the cries of people and strange creatures met her ears.

Should she trust him?

As she glanced out into the mêlée, she stared at the woman who had been attacked by what she could only describe as a vampire. She had no idea what she should do. She didn't know how to handle mythical creatures. Did you put a stake through a vampire's heart? Or was it silver bullets? Did they even have hearts? There was also something about garlic … and how did one fight off what she could only call a demon? She couldn't recall even one legend on how to stop a rabid werewolf … no, she was so far out of her league on how to survive something like this. The only thing she could think to do was crouch in the back bathroom and wait for morning.

Staring up at the angel again, she needed to put her faith in someone because at this point, she felt completely scared, alone, and lost.

He gazed at her intently. "Let me get you to safety."

Finally, it seemed her tongue worked. "How do you know my name? Who and what was that …

thing? What did he mean that when he said that you couldn't protect me?"

"There's time for all that later Bella, and I promise to tell you everything. For now, we need to get out of here. We must get away from this area."

He still held his hand out to her, and she met his gaze again. The feeling she knew him overcame her once more, and a little voice inside her whispered that she should trust him.

Placing her palm in his, she nodded.

"Is there a back door here?"

"Yes." She pointed toward the hallway behind the decimated display case.

"Let's go. Hopefully, the chaos hasn't moved outside the main town square, and we'll be able to leave without too much trouble. Is your home near here?"

"It's about a mile away."

"Okay. Please, stay close to me and do as I say."

Taking a deep breath, she followed him through the disarray that used to be her quiet, boring, unassuming life. How odd to think that just moments ago, she'd been wondering what she should do to put some excitement into it.

Never in a million years would she have chosen this.

END OF EXCERPT!

Please hop on over and purchase The Forbidden Knight. It's the next in the series, and you won't want to miss it!

www.ingramcontent.com/pod-product-compliance
Lightning Source LLC
Chambersburg PA
CBHW020611180626
46810CB00007B/2726